"I was hoping that maybe May would be out of rehab, and with the right amount of help, she would be able to take care of Isabella until I could get myself sorted out."

"Your leave is almost over," she said, as much to herself as to him.

"I know." Noah sighed again. "After tonight, I think I'm going to have to ask for an extension of my hardship leave. Things are just too complicated. I can't leave until all of the pieces are on the board."

"What can I do to help, Noah?"

"Will you go with me to see May in the hospital tomorrow?"

Both of them, Shayna believed, were aware that the kiss had changed things between them. But they were both also completely willing to ignore that big fat elephant in the room, sweep the issue right under the carpet and pretend like things were exactly the same as they always had been pre-kiss.

"Of course I will." For better or for worse, Noah Brand was still, at least for now, her best and oldest friend.

Dear Reader,

Thank you for choosing *The Marine's Christmas Wish*, the fifteenth Harlequin Special Edition book featuring the Brand family. *The Marine's Christmas Wish* is my first friends-to-lovers story; it was both challenging and fun to write.

Noah Brand is a career marine stationed overseas. When he receives an urgent message from his ex-girlfriend's mother with the news that he has a six-year-old daughter, Noah's world is turned upside down. Noah has to rely on his best friend, Dr. Shayna Wade, to help him navigate instant fatherhood. But it isn't until he sees Shayna dating another man that he realizes she is much more than his best friend—Shayna is his one true love. And making his best friend his winter bride becomes Noah's only Christmas wish.

Dr. Shayna Wade is an art history professor and a Christmas fanatic. Just as she's planning for her yearly Christmas light installation, an event that draws the notice of the local news and newspapers, Shayna's orderly life is disrupted by the appearance of six-year-old Isabella Millburn on her doorstep. With Noah on hardship leave from his overseas post, the three of them begin to forge a bond that feels to Shayna like a blossoming family. For Shayna, it's a dream come true—she has always loved Noah. But when her handsome personal trainer, Blake Forman, asks her out on a date, Shayna has to decide if she wants to keep Noah in the "friend zone" and open her heart to someone new, or if she should take a chance on happily-ever-after with the man she has loved her entire life.

Happy reading!

Joanna Sims

The Marine's Christmas Wish

JOANNA SIMS

HARLEQUIN
SPECIAL
EDITION

HARLEQUIN®

SPECIAL EDITION™

Recycling programs
for this product may
not exist in your area.

ISBN-13: 978-1-335-72423-6

The Marine's Christmas Wish

Copyright © 2022 by Joanna Sims

For questions and comments about the quality of this book,
please contact us at CustomerService@Harlequin.com.

Harlequin Enterprises ULC
22 Adelaide St. West, 41st Floor
Toronto, Ontario M5H 4E3, Canada
www.Harlequin.com

Printed in U.S.A.

Joanna Sims is proud to pen contemporary romance for Harlequin Special Edition. Joanna's series, The Brands of Montana, features hardworking characters with hometown values. You are cordially invited to join the Brands of Montana as they wrangle their own happily-ever-afters. And, as always, Joanna welcomes you to visit her at her website, joannasimsromance.com.

Books by Joanna Sims

Harlequin Special Edition

The Brands of Montana

A Match Made in Montana
High Country Christmas
High Country Baby
Meet Me at the Chapel
Thankful for You
A Wedding to Remember
A Bride for Liam Brand
High Country Cowgirl
The Sergeant's Christmas Mission
Her Second Forever
She Dreamed of a Cowboy

The Montana Mavericks: Six Brides for Six Brothers

The Maverick's Wedding Wager

Visit the Author Profile page
at Harlequin.com for more titles.

Dedicated to my husband.

Thank you for being my best friend and my muse.

I loved you yesterday. I love you today
I will love you always.

Prologue

"Don't look so sad, Shayna," Noah Brand said, his midnight blue eyes focused intently on her upturned face.

Shayna Wade had managed to keep her emotions under control on the drive from Sugar Creek Ranch to the Bozeman International Airport. But now, standing on the sidewalk after having watched Noah check in his marine-issued sea bag, Shayna felt like the tears she had been fighting might just win.

"This isn't goodbye," he told her as he folded her into his arms. "This is see you later."

"I know," she said with an emotional catch in her voice. "I know."

They had been best friends since they were kids and

they had been inseparable all the way until high school graduation. And even though Noah had moved away to attend college at Annapolis, this would be the first time that they would be a world apart from each other. Noah was to be a commissioned officer in the marines and was going to be stationed with the Third Marine Expeditionary Force in Okinawa, Japan. She would be staying in Montana to attend graduate school.

"Then, what is it?" He was holding her as tightly as she was holding on to him.

Shayna closed her eyes and tried to will away the world. She wanted to stay in Noah's warm, affectionate embrace forever; he had never held her this way before, and she was trying to commit every second of this moment to her memory so she could relive it again and again whenever she was missing him the most. The feel of his strong body so close to hers, the clean scent of his freshly pressed Marine Corps uniform and the feel of his heartbeat. She wanted to remember it all.

"Hey." Noah cupped his hand beneath her chin and lifted her face so he could see her eyes. "Shayna Wade doesn't let life get her down."

"No." She cleared her throat in an attempt to keep unshed tears at bay. "I don't usually."

As the only child of a single mother who worked nights, slept days and spent much of her free time in the local bars, Shayna had been forced to take on the parent role, to raise herself and take care of her mother as best she could. Her past had made her strong and independent. And she had learned at a very young age that crying didn't really get you anything other than a stuffy nose and puffy eyes. Even so, she couldn't stop a couple of tears from rolling down her cheeks.

"Hey." Noah pulled a monogrammed handkerchief from his pocket and wiped the tears off her cheeks. "None of that."

"I'm just going to miss you." She took the offered handkerchief, holding it tightly just in case more renegade tears made an escape. "That's all."

Noah smiled his wonderful smile; he had the whitest, straightest teeth that were the perfect companion for his straight nose, dimpled chin and golden skin. Noah Brand had always had leading-man good looks, and she, along with so many other Bozeman ladies, had loved him desperately for as long as she had known him. For her, as a young girl, it had been crush at first sight. But for Noah she had never been more than his faithful, ever-loyal best friend.

"I'll be back for a visit before you even have a chance to miss me." He smiled at her kindly, his arms dropping away from her shoulders.

She was about to protest when a notice on his phone drew his attention away from her. He looked at his phone, frowned and then kept on frowning as he shook his head.

"Still no word from her?" Shayna asked, tucking his handkerchief into the front pocket of her jeans.

"Nope." Noah tried to sound nonchalant, but she knew him too well.

"I'm sorry."

Noah and his high school sweetheart, Annika, had been arguing right up to his leave date. Instead of taking him to the airport as planned, Annika had never showed up and refused to answer Noah's text messages or phone calls. That was the reason that Shayna had been able to take Noah to the airport—to put off farewell for a few more precious hours. This had been Annika's moment with Noah to lose.

"Don't be." He took her hands in his and held on to them. "Women will come and go. A best friend is forever."

They both knew that *Annika* wasn't just any girlfriend—she was the love of Noah's life. She was the woman he had always intended to marry. No matter how many more romantic partners Noah had in his life, his love for Annika would always take up a big piece of real estate in his heart. In Shayna's mind, Noah and Annika would never be completely free from each other.

Noah smiled at her, but she could see in his eyes the pain he felt over Annika's rejection. "Who can I count on?"

"Me," she said with a half-hearted smile.

"Who have I always been able to count on no matter what?" Noah squeezed her fingers gently.

"Me."

"You." Noah nodded his head, his eyes locked with hers. "Always you."

They stood like that for several seconds, the world moving around them while they were locked in a private moment. Something odd flashed in Noah's eyes as he stared down at her; it was a look she couldn't read.

Noah reached out and tucked a strand of her hair behind her ear as he said, "I love you, Shayna. You know that, don't you?"

He had told her that so many times before, but this time she was certain that she detected a difference in his tone. Perhaps the distance that was soon to be between them was hitting him as well. Or perhaps he was simply missing Annika.

"I love you, too, Noah," she said and then closed her eyes, knowing that a kiss on her forehead, their standard goodbye, would soon follow.

Instead of feeling his lips on her forehead, she felt his large hands on either side of her face. Her eyes fluttered open just as Noah touched his lips to her lips. The moment their lips touched, she felt an electric spark jumped between them.

"Goodbye," he said softly, dropping his hands from her face.

She read in Noah's expression that he was as shocked by his own actions as she was.

"This isn't goodbye. Remember?" She finally broke the long, odd silence between them. "It's *see you later*."

"That's right, Shay." Noah lifted her hand and kissed it. "For us, it will never be *goodbye*."

Chapter One

Seven years later

It was nearly midnight on a late summer night in Montana when Captain Noah Brand arrived at his friend Shayna's home. He quickly tipped his Uber driver and rushed up the walkway to Shayna's 1930s Craftsman-style bungalow. At the top step of the broad wooden porch, the scent of vanilla from the clematis flower vines covering the square stone pillars brought memories of his childhood to the front of Noah's mind. Under the welcome mat, Noah found the key Shayna had left for him. Thank heaven for Shayna—no matter what curveball life threw at him, he could always count on her to be by his side. As Noah slipped the key into the lock, he was keenly aware of the fact that he needed Shayna now more than ever.

Noah quietly opened the door and entered the cozy world that Shayna had built for herself in his absence. Shayna, in his mind, was the phoenix rising from the ashes of her own troubled childhood to become a homeowner, a doctor of philosophy and an art history professor. She had really made something of herself.

Noah set his bag down gently just inside the front door; a giant, geriatric Great Dane by the name of Pilot lifted his large head and stared at him from his overstuffed bed situated near the fireplace.

"Shh." Noah lifted his finger to his lips.

Pilot, a recent adoptee Noah had met via video chat with Shayna, blinked at him several times before he groaned, stretched out his long legs and dropped his head back down into the fluffy softness of his custom bed. Noah quietly crossed the living room, seeming to hit every squeaky plank of the original wood floor. Pilot opened his eyes and lifted up his head again.

"Sorry to wake you, fella." Noah knelt down beside Pilot and petted him on the head. "Go back to sleep."

Pilot examined him with wizened black eyes before he dropped his head down, sighed happily and appeared to drift back to sleep.

"Softhearted Shayna," Noah whispered with a shake of his head. "Forever picking up strays."

Now safely past Shayna's version of a guard dog, Noah worked his way back to the master bedroom. He had never actually been to Shayna's house, but she had taken him on so many virtual tours that he believed he could find his way around the bungalow blindfolded.

Noah caught the strong scent of oil paints coming from the formal dining room; Shayna had always been an artist, and her favorite medium was oil. She had converted the formal dining room into her art studio because of the wall of floor-to-ceiling windows that flooded the space with the best light in the morning. The scent of oil paint drying on a canvas was a clue to Noah that Shayna had been painting early in the evening. Shayna painted when she was happy and inspired. But she also painted when she was upset or angry or worried.

Past the formal dining room and kitchen, Noah paused at the stairwell that led to the guest bedroom in the converted attic. He looked upward to the top of the stairs for a moment before he continued on his way down a narrow hallway that was lined with Shayna's favorite paintings she had created from the time she was a schoolgirl. One of those paintings was a portrait of him sitting on a fence at Sugar Creek Ranch, his family's cattle spread on the outskirts of Bozeman. Her talent always amazed him, and he was excited to see her new paintings. In fact, he had been tempted to take a detour into her converted dining room to check out the latest painting, but his need to see Shayna overtook his curiosity. Only Shayna could make him feel steady when his life began to feel like he was standing on shifting sands.

Noah paused in the doorway of the master bedroom.

He wanted to soak in the sight of his friend. Shayna had fallen asleep fully dressed, with her reading glasses on top of her head and a thick book of Impressionist painters still open by her side. Her fingers were stained with shades of purple and blue from the oil paints—the colors she chose usually reflected her mood. Was she in a dark mood because of him? He wouldn't be surprised. Life had just thrown him a curveball, and, of course, he had gone to Shayna first.

Noah smiled a bit when he saw a spot of white paint on the tip of her pert nose. Shayna always seemed to have paint on her hands, arms and face—he found it endearing. Her hair was longer than he remembered, and she had exchanged her black hair dye, a staple for years, for her natural shade of tawny brown.

Lost in thought, Noah was snapped back to reality by the Great Dane brushing past him. Pilot walked slowly, with a slight limp over to the bed, used doggy steps at the end of the bed to climb up onto the mattress and then dropped down beside Shayna. The giant dog rested his head on the empty second pillow, giving Noah the distinct impression that Pilot was claiming his spot next to Shayna.

Shayna began to stir at the weight of the massive dog jostling the mattress. Not wanting to startle her, Noah knelt down quickly by the side of the bed.

"Shayna." He whispered her name, gently touching her arm. "I'm here."

His friend's eyes fluttered open; she blinked at him as her striking green-and-gold cat eyes focused in on his face. Confusion and surprise gave way to happiness and love as she reached out her arms to hug him.

"Oh, Noah," she whispered. "Thank goodness you could come home."

Noah held on to her tightly, realizing that she was the only person in the world he wanted to see in that moment. It was lucky that he had graduated from Annapolis with the son of his immediate commander; Colonel Love had been able to arrange for Noah to have one-month hardship leave.

"Let's go outside where we can talk." She broke the embrace and put the book on the nightstand.

He stood up, held out his hand for her. Shayna took his hand and swung her legs off the bed. She was wearing a bohemian skirt, long and flowing, that danced around her ankles and brushed across the tops of her bare feet. Her toenails were painted lavender with tiny yellow and white daisies on each toe; the middle toe of her right foot was embellished with a white-gold infinity toe ring.

Shayna felt the top of her head for her glasses, untangled them from her long, fine hair and put them on top of the book. After he helped her to a stand, Noah followed her to a door that gave access to the fenced-in backyard from the master bedroom. They waited for the slow-moving old dog to gingerly work his way back down the steps and then walk, one plodding step after another, through the open door.

At the front of the house, he caught the sweet, comforting scent of almonds. In the backyard, there was a strong fragrance of lavender. Shayna had always dreamed of having a backyard where she could plant her flowers. It warmed his heart to see that she had made that dream, one of many, come true.

They walked together, arm in arm, across the plush, freshly cut lawn, to a whitewashed gazebo situated at the far end of the yard. The light from the sliver of a moon wasn't enough to dull the brilliance of the stars in the night sky like sparkling diamonds strewn across black velvet.

They sat on one of the wide benches in the gazebo facing the back of the house. Pilot joined them in the gazebo, resting his large frame near Shayna's feet.

Noah couldn't stop staring up at the spare bedroom window. In the dark of the night, he asked, "Do you think she's mine?"

For a split second, Shayna's body tensed next to his before she relaxed. There was an emotional undercurrent in her voice—perhaps no one but he would even have detected it—when she said, "Yes. I do."

Without even thinking, just reacting, Noah stood up, stepped forward as if his body wanted to run away from her words—and almost tripped over Pilot.

This couldn't be. It couldn't be. He had fought for years to evict Annika from his heart and vanquish thoughts of her from the deepest recesses of his mind.

He stared at the spare bedroom window for several moments longer before he turned back to Shayna. His eyes had adjusted to the dark, and he could see her features.

"She doesn't look like me." Noah wanted to make this point. For what reason, he wasn't sure. "She could be Annika's twin."

"Isabella has your smile," Shayna countered and there was a hint of accusation in her tone. "And your eyes."

"I'm not the only man in town with blue eyes, Shayna."

"That's true," she agreed softly. "Only you know if there's a chance that you could have fathered a child with Annika."

Noah ground his teeth several times, his jaw clenched, because he knew full well that there *was* a chance, however slim, that he could have made Annika pregnant. The last time they had been together, they had fought, they had made up; in the heat of the moment, passion had overtaken reason, and they had made love without protection. Annika had stopped taking birth control because she was having side effects, and neither of them had wanted to stop making love in order for him to run out to his truck and grab the box of condoms he had just purchased the day before. He had been young and in love, and he hadn't cared about the consequences. If he had gotten her pregnant, in his mind, Annika would agree to marry him instead of wanting to put off an engagement. It had been a no-risk proposition for him. He had always wanted to have a family with her. In fact, a pregnancy would have forced Annika's hand—he thought she would have had to marry him and move overseas.

Now, everything had changed. The idea of being

tied to Annika for the rest of his life infuriated him. The last time he had video chatted with her—and now he believed that she must have been in the early stages of pregnancy—she had told him, in stark, unemotional terms, that she had no intention of ever marrying him. After that, she had blocked him from all her social media, refused to take his calls or respond to his text messages, and that was when Noah had accepted that their tumultuous romance was officially over.

"There's a chance," he muttered as he rejoined her on the bench.

Shayna didn't respond, because his friend had already suspected that there was a chance—she knew him too well to think otherwise.

"Why would she do this?" Noah asked a question that he knew only Annika could answer. "Keep a child from me for all these years when she knew how much I wanted to be a…"

Noah's voice trailed off before he said the word *father* aloud.

"I don't know." Shayna's voice was steady and calm. "Annika has always been…"

"Unpredictable." Noah completed the thought. Annika's free spirit and irreverence for authority had hooked him from the very beginning. Even when they were in grade school, Annika had always pushed boundaries. She was forever finding herself in the principal's office, and he had loved her for it. But hiding a daughter from him? That was cruel. And he had never known Annika to be cruel. Thoughtless, yes, but never heartless.

"I still feel completely…"

"Shocked." She completed his thought, as they often did with each other. "Me, too. Annika's mother contacting me out of the blue and a babysitter dropping off a kid who could be yours. It's all so surreal."

Noah had to agree. Yes, Annika's mother, May Davis, knew Shayna. After all Shayna had grown up right across the street from Annika. Shayna had been a regular at May's table for dinner and often helped her with chores around the house to earn lunch money. But May and Shayna hadn't seen each other since Shayna's mother had died and Shayna sold the house she had grown up in. May had always been industrious; when she couldn't find a way to get in touch with him, she had tracked Shayna down at Montana State University. Noah didn't know all the details, and he didn't even know where Annika was now, but May had had custody of Annika's daughter, Isabella, for the last year. When May fell in her home and broke her hip, the babysitter was able to watch Isabella for a couple of weeks; May knew that a more permanent arrangement needed to be made while she was laid up in the rehab center. After scrolling through all her options, May had finally come to the conclusion that Noah would have to be contacted.

"I'm sorry." Noah took Shayna's hand in his. This wasn't the first time one of his dramas with Annika had landed in Shayna's lap. Admittedly, this was the biggest drama to date.

"Don't be." His friend held on to his hand. "You're

my best friend, Noah. And I believe that, no matter what the circumstances, a child is always a blessing."

"You're *my* blessing." Noah put his arm around Shayna's shoulders and then made an attempt to lighten the mood. "Saint Shayna."

"Not a saint," Shayna was quick to correct him. "I couldn't let Isabella get caught up in the system. I just *couldn't*."

Shayna had almost been placed in foster care several times, but her aunt and uncle stepped in and gave her a home. Her beloved aunt and uncle, now deceased, had thought about adopting Shayna, but that had never come to pass. With her own fractured childhood informing her adulthood, of course Shayna would identify with Isabella. It made sense.

They sat together in silence, Shayna's head on his shoulder, his arm around her, each caught up in their own thoughts. It was the quiet moments between them, each comfortable in the silence, that he appreciated the most. The sweetness in the cool night air reminded Noah of the last time he had ever seen Annika in person. If it were true, that he was a father and Isabella was his daughter, their last night together had produced a child. A daughter.

Pilot groaned as he stood up; he rested his heavy head across both of their laps.

"I think you're right." Noah said to the dog, petting the wiry gray hair around Pilot's head. "It's time to hit the rack—get some sleep."

With her hand tucked beneath his arm, Noah escorted Shayna back to the house. Once Pilot was installed back on her bed, Shayna led him across the hall to the ground-floor guest bedroom.

"I put clean sheets on the bed, and fresh towels are laid out in the bath down the hall."

Noah hugged her one last time, taking comfort in the familiar scent of her hair. Shayna was steady and strong. He needed that right now.

"Do you need anything else? I made you a plate of food from dinner—it's in the fridge."

"Thank you," he said, wondering how many times he would have to thank Shayna over the next several weeks. "I think I'm too tired to eat."

Shayna nodded wordlessly and turned to leave. In the doorway, she paused.

"Do your parents know you're in town?"

Noah unbuttoned the top button of his shirt. "No. Not yet."

He saw the concern on her face and shared it. His family was large and tight-knit; his mother, in particular, would be incredibly hurt if he was in town and hadn't come out to the ranch the moment he arrived.

"I need some time to think things through," he told her. "Before I involve them."

"It's a small town," Shayna pointed out.

As usual, she was right about that. Bozeman was too small to have big secrets.

"And your brother's wife owns the house right next door," she added.

"I just need a couple of days," he said wearily. "Then I'll open that can of worms."

He loved his family, but they were full of opinions and never hesitated to share them. He had joined the marines, in part, to be his own man and live his life on his own terms. It was a decision that had put the final nail in the coffin of his relationship with Annika. She'd wanted to keep her feet firmly planted on American soil, and he'd wanted to see the world—immerse himself in other cultures.

"Good night." Shayna said in a soft voice.

"Good night, Shayna." He watched her disappear into her bedroom and shut the door behind her. Moments later, the light in the master bedroom was turned off.

Noah quickly took care of his bathroom routine and then climbed into bed wearing boxers and a white undershirt. He was exhausted from his travels, but his mind wouldn't let him rest. Memories were all jumbled up with possible future scenarios. Noah stared up at the ceiling; for the first time since he had found out about Isabella, a little girl who could be his own flesh and blood, he felt something other than shock, fear, disbelief and anger. For the first time, he actually felt excitement. He could actually have a daughter. A *daughter*.

"Isabella," Noah said aloud. "Isabella is a beautiful name."

Shayna awakened just after dawn to let Pilot out. After her dog was taken care of and situated at his favorite spot in the living room, Shayna tiptoed up the stairs and peeked into the guest room. Isabella was still asleep, which gave Shayna an opportunity to quickly get dressed, check her emails and then prepare breakfast. She was accustomed to having her space to herself, so the appearance of a young girl was more than a disruption to her routine. Luckily, she had decided to not teach any summer classes so she could begin to write a textbook chapter on modern painters who worked in oils. Once Isabella was settled one way or the other, she would be able to get back to her routine.

While she was putting biscuits on a cookie sheet, she heard the downstairs guest room door open, and then, soon after, the guest bathroom door shut and the shower turned on. Noah was awake, and as it always did whenever she was near him, her heart began to beat a bit harder in anticipation. No matter how many times she had tried to convince her heart not to love him, she couldn't seem to break the habit.

"Morning." Noah emerged from the hallway looking crisp and refreshed. His short, military-style hair was combed in a precise manner, and his civilian clothes were still worn buttoned up and tucked in neatly. Noah now carried an air of dignity, strength and control in his lean, muscular frame. He looked like a military man now, exuded it, and it only added to his appeal.

"Good morning." Shayna pushed a steamy cup of black coffee toward him.

Noah sat down on one of the bar stools situated at

her large island and accepted the coffee with a look of gratitude on his handsome, freshly shaved face.

"She's not awake?" he asked after his first sip.

She shook her head while pouring her second cup of coffee.

Noah gulped down the rest of his coffee before he stood up. "I'm going to head out to see May and try to get some questions answered."

Shayna's eyebrows raised up and disappeared behind her long, bluntly cut bangs. "Practicing avoidance?"

Noah smiled sheepishly. "You bet I am."

Shayna believed that Noah had grown into his role as an officer; he was more mature now, more serious. Prior to the marines, Noah had always presented like an overgrown puppy—playful, mischievous and completely avoidant of responsibility. In the years since he had entered military service he had become a worldlier, more responsible man—of that Shayna was sure. But was he scared to death of meeting a six-year-old girl who might be his daughter? Absolutely. And who could blame him, really.

"She'll be awake when you get back." Shayna put his empty coffee cup in the sink.

Noah walked around to her side of the island and gave her a tight hug. "Can I borrow the Chevelle?"

To celebrate her job at the university, Shayna had purchased a mint-condition, forest green 1967 Chevy Chevelle. Shayna prized her muscle car and didn't let anyone else—other than him—drive it.

She smiled at him. "Keys are hanging up by the door."

Noah dropped a kiss on the top of her head, said thank you and headed toward the door. He grabbed the keys but hesitated in the foyer. He turned and looked at her.

"You look different."

Shayna touched her hair that was twisted into a haphazard bun on top of her head. "It's the hair."

"Maybe. But I think it's more than that." Noah opened the door. "I'll see you later."

"Play nice, Noah," she reminded him. Annika's mother and Noah hadn't always gotten along. May had believed that Annika's relationship with Noah had been too serious for high school kids. And there were several instances when Annika had sneaked out of the house to be with Noah.

"I'll do my best," Noah said before he walked out the door.

It wasn't long after Noah left that the smell of eggs and bacon and biscuits cooking in the oven lured Isabella out of bed. Still wearing her unicorn pajamas, her long, dark brown hair mussed, Isabella padded into the kitchen in her bare feet.

"Good morning, Isabella." Shayna smiled at the little girl. "Are you hungry?"

Isabella nodded as she climbed up onto the same stool Noah had recently occupied. The girl had been her guest for a couple of days, and Shayna noticed how quiet and reserved she was. Isabella nodded a lot but never had much to say, other than when she was talking to Pilot. With the geriatric Great Dane, Isabella was a total chatterbox.

"I hope you like scrambled." Shayna scooped some eggs onto a plate.

Isabella gave one definitive nod.

"Honey or jelly for your biscuit?"

Isabella pointed to the bottle of grape jelly.

"Bacon?" Shayna asked.

There was another nod yes.

She added a pat of butter on the biscuit before smearing on the grape jelly.

"Here you go." She put the plate in front of Isabella.

"Milk or orange juice?" Shayna asked, not giving her an option of pointing.

After a couple of moments, Isabella said in a near whisper, "Milk."

Shayna filled a glass with milk for her guest and put it down next to Isabella's plate with a napkin. She then put a small serving of scrambled eggs on her own plate, said a mental no to the biscuit and bacon, and poured herself a small glass of orange juice.

Shayna ate standing up instead of sitting down next to Isabella. Just like the last two mornings, it was a silent meal. Shayna knew not to push Isabella—the girl was in a strange house with an adult that she didn't know, and her grandmother was injured. Pushing Isabella could push her further into her shell. When people pushed Shayna when she was a kid, that's exactly what she did.

"It'll take her some time to warm up," May Davis had told her yesterday on the phone. "But once you get her started, you'll pray for a return to the quiet days."

"I want to see my nanna," Isabella whispered after taking a very large bite of her biscuit.

Shayna didn't make a big deal about it, but that was the first full sentence Isabella had ever spoken to her. "I know you do. And your grandmother wants to see you, too. As soon as she feels better, I will take you."

"I could stay with her," Isabella negotiated.

"When she gets better, both of you will go home," she said to the girl. "In the meantime, we could video chat with her again."

"Ok. But *I* can help her get better," Isabella said before she took another bite of her biscuit.

Shayna put her plate in the sink, grateful that Isabella seemed to have gotten over refusing to talk.

"As soon as the doctors tell your grandmother that she's ready to go home, I know you will do everything to help her."

"But when?"

Shayna nodded toward Isabella's plate. "Are you done? Do you want more?"

"But when?" Isabella ignored her questions.

"Sweet pea, I wish I knew."

Tears of frustration in her bright blue eyes, the little girl slid off the stool and ran over to Pilot for comfort.

Shayna cleaned the dishes and loaded them into the dishwasher, letting Isabella have her space. The more she interacted with Annika's daughter, the more she saw

Noah in her. And the thought of Noah having a child with his ex-fiancée made her feel incredibly sad and incredibly happy at the same time. She was happy for Noah that he would finally fulfill his dream of becoming a father—and she was also incredibly sad that her dream of being the mother of Noah's children, no matter how unrealistic, had been unceremoniously shattered by the arrival of Isabella on her doorstep.

Chapter Two

"Noah Brand." May Davis's voice was weak when she greeted him. "As I live and breathe."

May was propped up in her hospital bed in a semiprivate room. Luckily, there wasn't anyone occupying the second bed, which would allow them the opportunity to speak plainly about Isabella and Annika.

"Hello, May." Noah walked over to her bed.

"Well." May looked him up and down with eyes that were still sharp and keen despite her broken hip. "I never thought I'd see you again."

"That makes two of us."

May's eyes narrowed, and her arms crossed in front of her body. "Are you here to fight or clear the air?"

"I came to get some answers, May. That's all."

Knowing May, the only way he was going to get the answers he needed about Annika and Isabella was to be the one to extend the olive branch to her.

Noah held out his hand, close enough for her to reach. "Let's let the past stay in the past, May. That was a long time ago, and I don't have any beef with you."

May stared at his offered hand for several moments before she finally extended hers. The hand felt delicate and bony, with paper-thin skin marked with dark liver spots; May's once dark hair was snow-white and pulled back with a faded red, white and blue scrunchie.

"Well, then. Pull up a chair and take a load off." May waved her hand at a nearby chair as she pushed the tray with her breakfast, still mostly uneaten, away from the bed.

Noah pulled a nearby chair closer to the bed and then sat down. May's brown eyes were heavily lidded now, with deep wrinkles around her eyes and mouth and down her cheeks. He hadn't really noticed the passage of time when he was overseas, but now, seeing May's withered appearance, he realized that he had, in fact, been gone a long while. People had remained frozen in his mind—May, Annika and Shayna—but everything, and everyone, had changed in his absence. In a way, he had been living in a time warp.

"How are you feeling?" he asked to break the lengthy silence between them.

"Like hell," May said plainly. "My hip snapped just like an old chicken bone. Getting old ain't no picnic, I can tell you that much right now. They screwed me back together, put in some metal plates and rods. Heck, I'm darn near bionic at this point. Won't ever be able to get past the metal detectors at the airport." She shifted her weight a bit with a groan. "Not that I have anywheres to go necessarily."

May continued, "And let me tell you *another* thing—the surgery was the easiest part of this whole entire ball of wax! They transferred me to this rehab place from the hospital, and there's always somebody tugging on me or pulling on me. I don't know how anyone gets any sleep in this place. The therapists are the worst! *Torturists*, that's what I call them, right to their face."

"How long do they think you'll be in here?"

"Oh, heck," she said, turning her head toward the door and raising her voice loud enough for anyone who passed by her room to hear, "what do those doctors really know anyhow? I don't trust 'em—never have, never will. They say it could be a month before I'm back home. But if you ask me, it's all about the dollars." She rubbed her fingers together. "Once they stop making money off me, they'll boot me out of here quick as a hoot owl. I bet you that's the truth."

Noah nodded his head to let her know that he was listening to her, but his mind projecting ahead. It could easily be longer than a month that May would be out of commission. Once she did get home, taking care of a six-year-old wouldn't be manageable for her.

"Well, enough about me and my sad sack of suds. You didn't come here to listen to me whine and bellyache, now did you?" May stared at him intently. "Tell me, have you seen her?"

"She was asleep when I left to come here."

"She's just like Annika. The spitting image." May looked at him. He saw the look in her eyes change, and it was an emotion he had never seen before—remorse. "I didn't know she was yours right away, Noah. Give me a Bible and I'd swear to it. I suspected, but I didn't know for certain."

Noah suddenly felt sick to his stomach; it had never occurred to him, not once, that another man could be in the running to be Isabella's father. In his mind, he had always been the only option. May had just shredded that fantasy.

Noah tried to sound nonchalant. "Who did you think was the father?"

May frowned. "Jasper Millburn. Who else? Annika told me he was the daddy—put him on the birth certificate and everything. I asked her plenty about it, but she kept on swearing that Isabella was a Millburn, not a Brand."

He didn't answer right away; he needed a moment to collect his thoughts. "Do you think that Annika actually believed Isabella was Millburn's daughter?"

May looked away from him; when she looked back, Noah felt he had the answer without May saying the words aloud.

"Annika was known to tell a tall tale or two. But I can't say for sure that she knew it. The timing was right, you know. Jasper was sniffing around right after you went off on your big adventure."

Noah stood up and walked over to the window on the other side of May's bed. He rubbed his hand over his freshly shaved chin as he stared out at the cars in the parking lot. Annika had moved on from him pretty quickly with Millburn, a high school dropout and a first-rate troublemaker who had had more than his fair share of trouble with the law in Bozeman.

Still looking out the window, Noah asked, "If she was with Millburn right after I left, how do you know that she is mine, May?"

He didn't want to think it of May, but his family was the wealthiest in the Bozeman area. Could May be trying to secure her granddaughter's future by pinning paternity on him?

"DNA test." May's body stiffened, and her jaw set. "Jasper started to have his doubts."

Noah turned around to look at her face. "Why?"

"Those blue eyes. What else? She's got your eyes. Jasper and Annika both have brown eyes, but Isabella's eyes are as blue as the sky above. Not one Millburn has blue eyes. Not a one. So, he made Annika get a DNA test, and there's zero percent chance that Isabella is a Millburn. Zero."

"That doesn't make her mine, May," he said in a voice more calm than he felt inside. "If there was a Jasper, there could be a Tom or a Dick or a Harry."

May shook her head. "Go to that cabinet over yonder and get my purse." May's hand was shaking when she pointed. This visit would have to end soon; he was tiring her out, and his brain felt overloaded with new information.

Noah opened the nearby cabinet and found May's suede patchwork purse that she'd had when he first started dating Annika. May took the purse and began to riffle through it.

"I tote my important papers with me everywhere. Can't trust nobody, especially not the banks. What I'm about to show you is mighty important to me. It's proof."

May pulled a crinkled piece of paper out of the purse, unfolded it and then looked it over with a satisfied expression.

"Here." She held it out to him. "I did my own investigating last year. I didn't know if I'd find nothing but I sent away for one of those home find-your-kinfolk kits, and *that* will show you, plain as the nose on your face, why the father isn't no Tom, Dick or Harry. It's *you*. One of those little leaf thingies came up on Isabella's family tree, and when I clicked on it, guess whose name was on that little ol' leaf? It's right there in black and white. Do you see that? Bruce Brand. *Your* brother."

Noah focused his eyes on the part that listed his oldest brother as a relative. Bruce's wife, Savannah, must have talked him into researching the family tree—Bruce would never have done something like that on his own.

"Do you see that?" May asked again in a garbled voice. She coughed several times and cleared her throat.

Noah put the paper down on his lap but didn't have the words to respond.

"Whether you want her or not, Noah," May said defensively, "Isabella is *your* daughter."

He looked up from the paper and met May's eyes. "I want her, May, so get that thought out of your head. I've wanted Isabella all of my life. I just didn't know she was already here."

"Well, then. Good."

"I've got a lot of questions, May."

"I'm sure you do."

"But the biggest question I've got is…"

"Where's Annika?"

He nodded.

"She ran off with Jasper, that's what." May flicked her hand in disgust. "When the results came in, that good-for-nothing Millburn gave her an ultimatum."

"Isabella or him."

May had tears in her eyes—more from anger than sadness, he would suspect. She shook her head while she spoke. "My baby girl wouldn't choose no man over her own child if she hadn't been so screwed up."

May took her wallet out of her purse, opened it and showed him a faded picture of Annika in her gymnastics uniform. Annika had been a state-ranked gymnast with a full ride scholarship to several universities. Annika had decided to go to the University of Maryland so they could at least be in the same state during their college years. But, an accident during Annika's Junior year changed the course of both of their lives. Annika had been seriously injured while vaulting. After that, she never participated in gymnastics, and she lost her scholarship. May couldn't cover the cost for Annika, not even with financial aid, so Annika had dropped out of college and gotten a job as a waitress to make ends meet.

"Damn doctors," May said loudly, but then her voice lowered to nearly a whisper when she said, "They're the ones to blame. Got her hooked on those pills."

Suddenly, May was crying. Noah froze in his spot for a moment, seeing Annika's mother cry for the first time in his life. When he was able to move, he stood up and hugged her for as long as she would let him.

When she pushed him away, he grabbed some nearby tissues and handed them to her. May blew her nose several times before she said, "She wouldn't leave her baby, Noah. Not for nothing. She wouldn't."

"I know, May."

"When she couldn't get no more pills from the doctors…" Her voice trailed off.

"She went to Jasper."

May nodded. "For a while there, after she first left town, she called every week."

"When's the last time you heard from her?"

"It's been a good long while. Maybe six months?"

"Her phone?"

"Disconnected."

The older woman seemed to be shrinking before his eyes. Her skin looked ashen, and her voice was breathy and weak.

"I think that's enough for now, May." Noah stood up. "I'll come back to see you in the next couple of days."

May reached out for his hand; she looked up at him with a pleading look in her eyes. "Find her, Noah. Bring her home."

"I promise I will do what I can. For now, just get yourself better."

Noah was still sifting through all the information May had shared with him when he pulled into Shayna's driveway. He parked the Chevelle, turned off the engine and then sat behind the wheel, staring at the house in front of him. It was not lost on him that he was about to meet his daughter for the first time.

He had a daughter. And his daughter believed that her dad was another man.

"What a damn mess," Noah muttered. Annika had wanted him gone from her life so badly that she had convinced their daughter that Jasper Millburn was her father. What could have made her hate him that much?

It hurt. Bottom line—it hurt badly.

With a small bundle of items May had given to him tucked under his arm, Noah made his way to the front door. The sound of a little girl giggling caught his attention, and his standard military walk with purpose slowed until he came to a halt. Noah peeked through the space between the two tall, vertical fence boards and saw a slight girl with dark hair lying on her back with her head pillowed on Pilot's broad body.

Isabella. She was looking up at the blue sky, talking

to Pilot in an animated fashion and then giggling as if she had just told him a very funny joke.

Mesmerized by the sight of his daughter, Noah watched her for a couple of seconds longer before he pulled himself away. At the front door, Noah paused, pressed the thumb and forefinger of his free hand into the corners of his eyes, and gave himself a moment to collect his emotions. He had been robbed of the privilege of greeting Isabella when she came into the world; he had been robbed of hearing her first cry or her first word. He hadn't been able to see her walk for the first time or tuck her in bed at night. These were priceless moments never to be recovered.

But the first sound he had heard from his daughter was her giggling happily as the sun shone down on her face. And there was something incredibly precious about that.

By the time Noah opened the door, he felt in control of his emotions once again. He unlocked the door, opened it and then hung up the keys. He found Shayna sitting in a chair in her art studio looking through her Christmas binders. Her chair, he noticed, was situated perfectly so she could keep a watchful eye on Isabella. There was a brief moment, similar to the moment he had just experienced with Isabella, when Noah was able to observe Shayna before she looked up and noticed him standing in the doorway. The light streaming in from the large bay window had painted a soft yellow stripe along the middle of the mahogany wood of the long table. This same light was filtering through a period

stained-glass accent window, and there was a kalei-
doscope of jewel-tone colors dancing across Shayna's
cheek and neck. He had always thought she was attractive in her own way, but in this light, in this moment,
he realized that Shayna Wade was beautiful.

"Oh!" Shayna said with a surprised laugh. "I didn't
hear you come in."

The spell was broken, and Noah walked forward
to join her. Shayna closed the binder she was looking
through and gave him her full attention. She moved her
tortoiseshell-rimmed glasses to the top of her head; her
unruly, wavy hair framed her face in a way that emphasized the brightness of her green eyes.

"Tell me everything," she said, pointing to a chair
beside her.

Noah sat down and handed his friend the bundle of
items May had given him. Shayna looked at him and
then the bundle.

"Open it," he told her, feeling tired, both from jet lag
and from his lengthy discussion with May.

Shayna opened the crumpled manila envelope and
pulled out the items inside. The first item Shayna unfolded was the ancestry papers; she studied them carefully, and then he saw her face blanch before the color
returned to her cheeks. Shayna folded the papers and
rested her hands on top of them, her eyes meeting his.

"She's yours."

He had to swallow hard several times before he said,
"It looks that way."

His friend gave a little nod as her eyes drifted away;

it was quick, but he saw an odd, inexplicable sadness in her hazel-green eyes.

"What's this?" Shayna put the papers back inside the envelope and exchanged them for a small, thread-bare photo album.

"Isabella as a baby."

The spine of the photo album made a cracking sound when Shayna opened it. The first picture she came to was one of Annika in the last stages of her pregnancy. On the opposite page, there was a picture of Annika holding Isabella moments after her birth.

"She looks happy," Shayna said quietly before she closed the photo album and handed it back to him. "I'll look at this later."

Noah nodded. He hadn't made it through the entire album, either.

"Did she tell you anything about Annika? Where is she?"

"We discussed Annika." He nodded, his eyes focused on the little girl in the yard.

Shayna raised her eyebrows at him with a question mark in her eyes when he didn't immediately begin to fill her in about what he learned about Isabella's mother.

"I just—" he started, then stopped, readjusted his thoughts, and said, "I'd rather not get into it right now."

Shayna, as always, didn't press him. She knew that, in time, he would tell her everything. She put her hand over his, squeezed and said, "Then I think it's time for you to meet your daughter, Noah."

"Agreed."

His friend smiled at him kindly. "You look terrified, Captain Brand."

"Do I?"

Shayna broke the tension with a laugh and a smile. "She's just a little girl, Noah."

She was right—Isabella was just a little girl. And, in this moment, that little girl with the dark brown hair and blue eyes—so much like his own—scared the daylights out of him. He didn't know why—he just *was*.

"Come on." Shayna stood up with another sweet laugh. "I think you're exactly what she needs right now. And maybe she's exactly what *you* need right now."

Noah stood up as well, and together they walked to the door that led out to the backyard. What did a father say to his daughter for the first time, particularly when she didn't know that he was, in fact, her father?

Shayna opened the door and called out, "Isabella! Come and meet a friend of your nanna's."

Isabella's dark head popped up, as did Pilot's. Isabella rolled upright and bounced to a stand. She waited patiently while Pilot groaned and creaked his way standing. His daughter looked so slight and fragile walking next to the old, graying Great Dane. Her kindness for the elderly dog touched his heart.

"So much like her mother."

"Yes," Shayna agreed.

Everything Noah had thought about his life prior to this very moment was washed away as Isabella slipped her hand into his.

"Hi," he said to her, giving her hand a gentle shake. He resisted the urge to scoop her up and hug her.

"Hi," she said cheekily, staring up at him with wide, intelligent eyes.

Isabella was an earthquake that had just shaken the foundation of his life. Nothing after today would ever be the same. Every decision he made about his career, about his life, would have to be viewed with his daughter in mind.

"What's your name?" she asked, her head tilted, staring at his face curiously.

"Noah." He was struck by how much Isabella resembled her mother. And yet, he could see himself in her face. The cleft in her chin, the shape of her lips and yes, of course, those bright, sapphire-blue eyes. Those were Brand eyes. "What's yours?"

"Isabella May Millburn."

The last name hit him like a punch in the gut. She had the wrong last name, and he wasn't going to let that stand. She was Isabella Brand—the name, the family fortune, the family legacy were hers by birth, and she wouldn't be denied any of it.

"Nice to meet you, Isabella."

His daughter seemed to be fascinated with his face but didn't say anything in response.

"Are you hungry?" Shayna asked. "Ready for some lunch?"

Isabella nodded her head silently; then, to his absolute surprise, she slipped her hand back into his and held it as they headed inside. He caught Shayna's eye over

Isabella's head; there were unshed tears in his friend's eyes. Shayna's happiness for him endeared her to him in a new, unexpected way. It had seemed impossible that he could love Shayna any more than he already did, and yet, in that single moment, his heart swelled with more love for her than he had ever felt before in his life.

As he walked hand in hand with his daughter, Noah was certain that this was one of those moments in his life that would be forever seared into his brain. The tinkling, lilting sound of her voice, the feel of her small, smooth hand encased so trustingly in his, and the look in her eyes the first time she saw—unknowingly—her father's face. Without any doubt, Noah knew that he loved her—instantly, instinctively and innately. Isabella May was his daughter; now, and for the rest of his days, a very important piece of his heart belonged to her.

Some bonds could not be denied. Shayna watched Noah and Isabella begin their relationship, and the connection between them formed quickly and easily. Unlike with her, Isabella didn't whisper when she talked with Noah, and she used more words than nods and gestures.

"You saw my nanna today?" Isabella asked between bites of her peanut butter and banana sandwich.

Noah nodded.

"When do *I* get to see her?"

"Next week."

"But *why*?" his daughter whined.

"She wants to feel a little bit better, that's all." Shayna explained.

"*You* don't know." Isabella said angrily, "You don't know anything!"

This was the first flare of anger she had seen in Isabella, but she doubted it would be the last. She had, in the blink of an eye, lost her home, her grandmother and her security. And this was, of course, after her mother and father had disappeared from her life the year before.

"Isabella." Noah's tone was more abrupt than he had intended.

"She *doesn't*," the girl responded. "Why do I have to stay here? I want my mom. I want my dad. If you call them, they'll come get me."

Shayna watched Noah work hard to keep his expression and his tone neutral. "Your mom is hiking with your…dad… Until we can get in touch with them, you can hang out with us. And Pilot. We're cool people, don't you think?"

Isabella threw her half-eaten sandwich on the plate and wordlessly went to lie down next to Pilot on his bed. Shayna and Noah exchanged a look.

After she cleaned up the dishes from lunch, Shayna waved her hand for Noah to follow her out of Isabella's earshot. Yes, she already felt overwhelmed by the situation, but she needed to know what Noah had found out about Annika and Jasper.

Once they were alone in the hallway, Shayna whispered, "What did you find out from May, Noah? *Where* is Annika?"

Chapter Three

Noah was careful to keep his naturally loud voice quiet enough that his daughter wouldn't be able to hear his words. "May doesn't know. That's the bottom line. Annika followed Millburn to some hippie commune in Colorado. He had visions of grandeur."

"Meaning?"

"He believed he was going to make his fortune growing marijuana."

"Lord."

"The last contact May had from Annika was over six months ago."

"Her cell phone?"

"Disconnected."

Shayna leaned back against the wall and bit her lip in

thought. "I just can't believe this, Noah. Annika hasn't contacted her daughter in *six months*?"

Noah shook his head no.

"How could she?" Shayna felt queasy as she caught Noah's eye. "Drugs?"

He nodded.

Instinctively, she reached out to hold his hand. "What are you going to do?"

"I'm going to track her down." Noah said firmly. "And then I'm gonna bring her home."

"What if she won't come?"

There was a steely determination in her best friend's eyes. In the low light, they had turned a stormy shade of blue. "She'll come. One way or another."

"And Jasper?"

"If he's smarter than I give him credit for, he'll stay the hell out of my way."

"If you're going to stay here and eat my food, you're going to pull your own weight," Shayna said to Noah's daughter.

Isabella's eyebrows drew together. "What does that mean?"

"It means," Shayna said after she had finished washing the lunch dishes, "that *you* are going to help me get my Christmas boxes down from the attic."

"Christmas?" The little girl rolled her eyes as if it was the silliest thing she'd ever heard. "I'm not even back in school yet."

"So?" Shayna wiped her hands on the dish towel before folding it over the kitchen sink.

Isabella continued to frown at her. "So. It's not time for Christmas."

"It is for me."

"That's weird." Isabella sat down on the couch with her arms crossed in front of her.

"It's not weird to love Christmas."

Noah walked into the room. "What's this I hear about Christmas?"

"She thinks it's time for Santa Claus."

"Who says it's not?" Noah asked.

Isabella lifted up her arms and dropped them down beside her body in frustration. "It's not time yet!"

Noah sat down next to Isabella on the couch. "Who says we can't have Christmas in June, or July, or September for that matter?"

"Santa," Isabella shot back. "Duh."

Shayna grabbed a sizable binder from a nearby bookshelf, brought it over to a large, thickly woven rug in front of the couch and sat down cross-legged with the binder in front of her.

"Santa *loves* my Christmas display," she told the girl. "We're tight like that."

Isabella looked skeptical. Shayna didn't pay any mind to her attitude. Once Isabella got a look at the pictures of her yearly Christmas extravaganza, she would get caught up in the wonder of Christmas. For Shayna, tapping into Christmas filled her with joy, no matter what time of year it was.

"Every year," Noah explained, "Shayna puts up an amazing Christmas display in her front yard. It's a really big deal."

Isabella still looked unimpressed.

"She gets her picture in the paper and even gets on TV."

"I guess that's kinda cool."

"Why, thank you, Isabella." Shayna laughed. "I think it is kinda cool myself."

Shayna patted the rug next to her and said, "Come here and take a look at what I've done in the past."

Isabella slipped off the couch, took a couple of skips toward her and then fell to her knees onto the rug. She sat with her legs in a W formation. In that moment, Isabella so resembled her mother that it whisked Shayna back in time to the first moment she had ever met Annika, in first grade. Annika had been new to Bozeman, and anyone new felt like an exotic creature from a mystical land. All the boys were attracted to her and swarmed around her on the playground like bees to honey. But there wasn't a boy in their class who was more smitten with Annika than Noah.

"First grade," Shayna said out loud, and when Isabella gave her a curious look, she realized she had been staring at the little girl at her side.

"I'm going to be in first grade," Isabella said.

Shayna met Noah's gaze over the dark head of his daughter. There was a question in his eyes that made her break the connection.

"I want to see the pictures," Isabella said impatiently.

"Please," Noah and she said in unison.

"Please," the little girl mimicked with a hint of sarcasm.

"We're going to have to work on your manners a bit," Shayna said to the girl.

"Okay." Isabella tilted her head to the side. "Nanna says the same thing all the time."

Shayna opened her binder to the first page to show Isabella her first Christmas display. She had always wanted to put up decorations at Christmastime, but her mother had said that there wasn't enough money. One year, when she was close to Isabella's age, her aunt and uncle brought over a little Christmas tree with twinkling blue lights. They had even bought and wrapped presents so there would be something for her to open on Christmas morning. Shayna could remember, as if it were yesterday, how excited she had been on Christmas Eve. So excited, in fact that she hadn't been able to sleep at all. And because she couldn't sleep, she was awake when her mother came home, intoxicated, and stomped all over her Christmas presents. No matter how many years passed, Shayna's brain always seemed to go back to that moment in time.

"Wow! You put all of this stuff up?" Isabella asked her.

The question brought her out of her own musings and into the present moment. "Yes. I did. The first couple of years, I did it all by myself."

Shayna flipped to the next page. "But once it made the newspapers—" Shayna pointed to the newspaper article "—and more and more people came to see my displays, I needed help."

"Who helps you?"

"Students from the university, mainly."

Noah chimed in, "Dr. Shayna Wade."

Isabella tilted her head with a curious look on her face. "You're a doctor?"

"Well, not the kind of doctor you go to when you're sick or have a broken arm," she answered.

"What kind, then?"

"I'm a doctor of philosophy."

"What does that mean?" Isabella scrunched up her face in the cutest way. In that moment, Shayna felt nothing but love for the little girl with Noah's bright blue eyes.

"It's hard to explain," she told her. "I'm an art professor, so I know a whole lot about art."

"I don't know what that means."

Shayna laughed. "That's okay. I'm not sure I understand, either."

They flipped through more pages of her binder, and with each display, Isabella seemed to become more excited.

"I try to have a theme every year. Last year, it was the Island of Misfit Toys, and this year, it was Santa's reindeer. The displays just got bigger and bigger…"

"And bigger!" the girl exclaimed, bouncing up onto her knees excitedly, her bottom resting on her heels.

"That's why I have to start so early. It takes a lot of planning," she explained.

"What are you going to do this year?" Noah's daughter asked.

"I was thinking about Frosty the Snowman. But I'm not one hundred percent sure about that."

Suddenly, Isabella bounced up, ran around the room in a little circle and then executed a perfect handstand, confirming that she was, indeed, Annika's daughter. Breathlessly, her eyes shining, her cheeks flushed, Isabella exclaimed, "I have an idea!"

Shayna and Noah exchanged another look. Isabella had gone from skeptic to enthusiast in record time.

"Lay it on me," Shayna said, closing her binder.

"Princesses! You could have Elsa from *Frozen*, Ariel, Belle, Jasmine!" Isabella waved her arms in the air. "We could make all of them!"

"We?" Noah asked.

"Well, you are a really good carpenter," Shayna reminded him.

It was at that moment that Shayna realized that this Christmas display would be the first holiday moment Noah ever had with his firstborn. It was more than just building a display—it would be building a forever memory that Isabella would carry in her heart for the rest of her life.

"All right." Shayna nodded. "*Princesses* it is."

Isabella did another handstand, walked on her hands toward Pilot's bed and then dropped her feet back to the ground, ran the rest of the way to Pilot and slid across the carpet on her knees.

"Pilot!" Isabella said to the elderly canine. "Guess what?"

"We've got to get that girl into gymnastics." Shayna stood up and scooped up her binder. When she looked back at Noah, he had a concerned look in his eyes.

"What?" She asked him.

"Shayna, I'm not going to be here for Christmas. I've only got leave for four weeks, then I go back."

"I know," she whispered. "But you're here now. Before you came, I couldn't get her to say hardly two words. Now she's got plenty to say. I don't think that's a coincidence. I think it's because of you."

"But your Christmas display, Shayna," he said. "You look forward to it every year. I know you don't want to really do Disney princesses."

"No. I don't. But what's going on here is important." She lowered her voice. "More important than any theme I might want. This is something she can do with you, even if it is only for a couple of weeks."

"You're the best, Shayna." Noah stood up, crossed to where she was standing and folded her into his arms.

"That darn binder is in my way," he complained.

She laughed, gave him a quick hug in return and then stepped back a bit so she could smile up at him with genuine love and affection in her eyes. "We've looked out for each other our whole lives, haven't we?"

"Yes, we have," he said with a small, self-effacing grin. "But you got the short end of the stick on that one, I'm afraid."

"I always knew you were Peter Pan, Noah. Even when we were kids, I knew."

"I can't be Peter Pan forever." Noah admitted, "I have to grow up."

"Yes, Noah," she agreed. "You really do."

Noah was looking at her as if he had never truly seen her before. His examination of her face, her features, her eyes—his gaze was so intent that she felt her cheeks and neck begin to flush.

"Why are you looking at me like that?" she asked with a nervous little laugh that irritated her the moment it came out. She wasn't a giddy schoolgirl anymore, and she shouldn't sound like one, especially with Noah.

"I don't know. You're different, somehow. Your hair, the way you hold yourself. Even your smile… Wait a minute! What happened to the gap in your front teeth? I loved that little gap."

"You're just noticing that now?"

"I've been a bit distracted." Noah glanced over at Isabella, who was still talking Pilot's ear off about Disney princesses.

"Touché," she said and then added, "I've made some changes."

He looked at her so seriously and intently when he said, "I'm not sure I like the changes you've made."

When Noah looked at her like he was looking at her now, it made her feel self-conscious and unsure of herself—two feelings she did not like. To cover up how she was actually feeling, Shayna gave a sassy little shrug and started to walk over to the bookcase to put her binder back in its place. On her way, she tossed over her shoulder, "Well, I guess it's a good thing it's not up to you."

Noah hadn't realized just how much Christmas stuff Shayna had in her attic. The storage space was organized, but it was hot. One by one, the three of them hauled the Christmas boxes downstairs to the first level and stacked them neatly in the formal living room, where Shayna always put her biggest Christmas tree. Shayna had many trees in the attic—all shapes and sizes, and in many different colors. It seemed to Noah that there wasn't a Christmas tree for sale that Shayna wouldn't buy and bring home.

"Is this all of it?" Noah asked, wiping the sweat off his brow with the bottom of his T-shirt.

"Need a break, Marine?"

"Heck yeah," he said, wiping off fresh beads of sweat. "I need water and food."

"Me, too." Isabella was lying flat on her back next to the boxes.

"We've done enough for today, I suppose," Shayna said, slumping into an overstuffed wing-back chair nearby. "The rest is in the attic above the garage. We can do that later."

"I love how you always say *we*," Noah complained as he lay down on a nearby couch.

Pilot wandered into the room and groaned as he lowered his large body down next to Isabella.

"I can't believe you do this every year," Noah said.

Shayna twisted her long, thick hair into a bun on top of her head, holding it in place while she fanned her neck with her other hand. "Sometimes I can't, either. It's a labor of love."

Isabella curled her body to the side so she could hold on to one of Pilot's paws.

The three of them rested in silence for a while, and Shayna even thought that Noah had dozed off when a knock at the front door interrupted the moment.

Noah sat upright. "Are you expecting anyone?"

She shook her head with a frown. "No. But I did order some more buildings for my Christmas village."

Shayna ignored the stiffness in her back when she stood up; she walked over to the door and looked through the peephole.

Colt!

She spun her head around, eyes wide, and mouthed the name *Colt* to Noah. Colt Brand was Noah's brother, and he just happened to be married to her best friend and next-door neighbor, Lee Macbeth. During the pandemic, Colt and Lee had been living at Sugar Creek Ranch with their newborn son, Jock.

Noah had parked her Chevelle in the driveway—Colt knew her well enough to know that she wouldn't leave her prized muscle car in the driveway if she weren't home. She waved her hand at Noah to signal for him to stay put.

"Colt!" Shayna swung open the door with a broad smile pasted on her face.

"Hey, Shayna." Colt tipped his Stetson cowboy hat in greeting. Colt was taller than Noah, and he wore his hair longer, but they looked so much alike in the face that they could be mistaken for twins.

Shayna peeked over his shoulder. "Is Lee with you?"

"Naw." Colt rested his foot on her threshold. "She's back at the ranch with the baby."

"I've missed having her next door. I feel like I never get to see her anymore."

"I tell you what, she's really missed you," Colt drawled. "We appreciate you keeping an eye on the place, though."

"Of course."

There was a moment of silence between them, and Shayna felt that Colt was expecting for her to ask him to come in. After that awkward couple of seconds, Noah's brother said, "Lee's ready to move back home."

"That's wonderful!" Shayna said sincerely. Lee was her best friend, and it had been such a long time since she had been able to just walk next door to catch up with her.

"I suppose." Colt pushed the brim of his hat up, making his Brand blue eyes—so much like Isabella's and Noah's—easier to see. "I've been plenty happy at Sugar Creek."

"I'm sure."

"But I want Lee to be happy, and she's homesick for her place."

"When are you moving back?"

"Maybe three or four weeks from now. That's her plan, and I'm just gonna go along with it. Happy wife, happy life."

"Well—" Shayna smiled at him, hoping that he would take a hint that she was busy "—I'm looking forward to having you back in the neighborhood. Let me know if there's anything I can do to help."

"Will do." Colt gave her a bit of an odd look, but he tipped his hat at her to signal that he was getting ready to take his leave.

"And I can't wait to get my hands on that baby." She began to close the door with a little wave.

Colt smiled with the pride of a new father. "He's something. Really something."

She nodded her agreement. "Good seeing you, Colt."

"Same to you." Colt tipped his hat to her again and was just about to turn around when Isabella appeared at her side.

Colt stopped and stared at the little girl while Shayna's heart slammed into overdrive and her armpits started to sweat.

"Hi," Isabella said matter-of-factly.

Colt's eyes bounced from Isabella to Shayna and then back to the little girl.

"Howdy," he responded.

Darn it! It had almost been a clean getaway.

While Shayna was searching her brain for something normal to say by way of explanation of the sudden appearance of a child in her house, Isabella filled the gap and said to Colt, "How come you look like Noah?"

* * *

"You had no idea?" his brother Colt asked him.

They were in the backyard with Pilot while Shayna kept Isabella occupied opening the Christmas boxes.

"No. I didn't. How would I? Annika blocked me and the family from all of her social media. None of her friends would talk to me. It was frickin' radio silence for years. Heck, I didn't even know she had a kid, much less *my* kid."

"Damn, brother," Colt said. "This is some serious stuff."

"I know."

After a lull in the conversation, and after his brother seemed to process the shock of having a surprise niece, Colt asked, "When are you going to let Mom and Dad know you're in town *and* that they have another grandchild?"

"Soon."

"Heck yeah, soon. If anyone sees you here…" His voice trailed off.

"I know. I know," Noah said. "But all of this just landed in my lap. I need some time to figure it out before I open the floodgates of our family."

"I hear that." Colt laughed. "Lee is always telling me our family is extra."

"Damn straight they are," Noah said. "That's why I just need to get some things straight—get a lawyer, hire a private detective to track down Annika and Millburn."

"What was she thinking with that guy?"

Noah almost didn't utter his next word, but this was

his brother, and he knew he could trust him to keep family business in the family.

"Drugs."

Colt let that information soak in for a moment. With a shake of his head, he said, "I was afraid of that."

They continued to catch up for a while before Colt said he needed to get back to the ranch before the baby woke up. They both headed inside Shayna's house. Colt pulled out his phone, unlocked it and then handed it to Noah so he could see his screenshot.

"Man. He's gotten big," Noah said of Colt's son, his nephew.

"Junior can put some food away." Colt laughed taking his phone back.

Even though Colt's son was a second, after his grandfather, the family just found it easier to call him Junior.

"I can't wait for you to meet him," Colt said, ducking his head to stop the bright sun from hitting his eyes. "You've been overseas his entire life."

"Hard to believe."

His brother looked over at him when they reached the back door of the house. "You have a daughter."

Noah nodded. He knew it in his mind, but it hadn't fully sunk into his heart. One minute he was thrilled to be Isabella's dad, and the next he dreaded the complications having a daughter with Annika would most likely bring.

"You're a father." Colt gave him a hug and patted him hard on the back a couple of times. "Congratulations, man. I mean it. This is a blessing."

"That's what Shayna called it. A blessing."

"And she's right," Colt retorted easily with grin. "As usual."

Noah's lips thinned, but he didn't respond; he was conflicted about the whole thing and still in shock. Yes, he wanted to be a father. But he'd worked for years to scrub Annika from his mind and his heart, and now here she came, taking a wrecking ball to the wall he had so painstakingly built between them.

Pilot had sauntered over to the back door and was waiting patiently for them to let him back in to rejoin Shayna and Isabella.

"Annika never makes anything easy, does she?" his brother commented while they headed back inside, walking slowly side by side.

"No."

Colt lowered his voice a bit. "Sounds like the thrill is gone."

Noah got his meaning—his family didn't like him with Annika. They had always had a volatile roller-coaster ride of a relationship, and the Brand family in its entirety did not approve of them as a couple.

"Long gone, brother," Noah reassured him. "Long gone."

Chapter Four

"Is that Santa?" Isabella was sitting back on her heels, impatiently waiting for Shayna to unwrap an enormous Santa candle.

Shayna smiled and put the candle carefully on the coffee table. "Smell it."

Isabella leaned forward, breathed in deeply, and while she breathed out, her eyes widened happily. "It smells like a candy cane!"

Shayna touched the candle lovingly. "That's my favorite part."

Isabella ran her fingers over the shiny red Santa suit, stopping at each coal-black button. "Are you ever gonna light him?"

"No," she said, reaching into the box for a second candle. "Never. I'm going to keep him forever."

"Okay." The little girl was noticeably disappointed.

"Look at this one." Shayna unwrapped the second candle figurine. "Frosty the Snowman."

Again, Isabella's ocean-blue eyes, which appeared to Shayna to be even brighter than Noah's because of her dark brown hair, widened with wonder. The look in this child's eyes was exactly the reason why she worked so hard on her Christmas display every year. No matter what was going wrong in a child's life, the magic of Christmas, even if was just for a second or two, could transport a person from their sadness and deliver them a moment of joy. That's exactly what Christmas had done for her in her adult life.

"What does he smell like?" Isabella asked.

"You tell me."

Noah's daughter leaned forward and took a big whiff of the candle.

"Well?" Shayna asked.

Pure delight registered on Isabella's face. "Is it marshmallow?"

Shayna smelled the snowman and then hugged him to her body. "Marshmallow."

"I love them," Noah's daughter said earnestly.

"So do I."

Without warning, Isabella leaned over and hugged her. That one hug touched Shayna in an unexpected way. She returned the hug, hoping that this would be the first hug of many to come. Christmas made them both happy, and it was something that they shared.

With Frosty safely placed on the table next to Santa,

Shayna proceeded to unwrap a set of smaller candles that featured Santa in his sleigh being pulled by his reindeer, with Rudolph the red-nosed reindeer at the front of the team.

"Why do you love Christmas so much?" Isabella asked her.

"Well—" Shayna stopped unpacking the box in front of her, knowing that there was an unvarnished version and a varnished version. She would share the latter with Isabella. "When I was just a little girl, not much older than you, really, my mom couldn't afford to give me a Christmas."

"No Christmas?" Isabella's dark brown eyebrows drew together in surprise.

Shayna opened the next box. "No Christmas. We just couldn't afford it."

"No Christmas?" the young girl asked again, as if she was confirming that she had heard it correctly. "That's super sad."

"It was sad," Shayna agreed honestly. "I always promised myself that when I grew up, I would have the best Christmases anyone had ever seen. And every year, I do. So, it isn't sad anymore. And, really, I get to share my Christmas with anyone who wants to come by my display."

"And this year will be the happiest year because we will have princesses?"

Shayna laughed at the girl's laser focus on the princesses. "Absolutely."

Isabella carried empty boxes over to the corner of

the living room. When she returned, Shayna had un-wrapped one of her prized items from her Christmas village.

"Look." Shayna finished unwrapping the tissue paper and revealed a large, porcelain Christmas tree with strings of vibrant multicolored lights, round, shiny silver ornaments and a gold star at the top. The tree sat on a snowcapped base that read Merry Christmas. "This is the crown jewel of my Christmas village."

"Does it light up?"

"Well, of course it does," she said. "I wouldn't dream of having a Christmas tree in my village that didn't light up."

"Can we light it up now?"

That made Shayna laugh again with pure joy; usually she unwrapped her Christmas regalia alone. Unpacking it with Isabella was so much better.

Together, they moved over to the nearby end table; Shayna placed the tree on the table and then plugged it into the light socket. Isabella rested her chin on the arm of the couch, her face alight with anticipation.

"Ready?" Shayna asked.

Isabella nodded.

The Christmas tree was turned on, and the strings of lights flashed red, then blue, then green. The glittery gold star glowed brightly at the top of the tree.

"Do you like it?"

"Oh, yes." Isabella appeared mesmerized by the tree. "I do."

"And so it begins." Noah entered the living room with Colt. "The ever-growing Christmas village. How many buildings do you have now?"

"Not nearly enough," Shayna said without hesitation. She stood up and smiled at the brothers. "I want to build a shelf all around this living room and fill it with the most amazing village anyone has ever seen."

"If anyone can do it, you can," Colt said encouragingly. Then, he added, "Lee told me you've been working out with Blake."

"Blake? As in Blake Foreman?" Noah piped in. "The super-scrawny kid who always got shoved into the gym lockers?"

"You've been gone awhile, brother. No one's gonna shove Foreman anywhere anymore. Not unless they want to get shoved back into next week," Colt said before Shayna had a chance to defend her personal trainer.

Shayna tugged at her Montana State University T-shirt and glanced quickly at Noah before she answered. "I've been working with for him for a while now."

"Whatever you're doing, it's working," Colt said.

Out of the corner of her eye, she could see Noah's gaze sharpen on her.

"Thank you. He's a really great guy."

Colt gave a nod, then put his hat back on. "Tell him I still owe him that beer."

"I will."

She had always been heavyset as a child, and that had persisted into adulthood. Food had been scarce in her home at times—sometimes her mom would forget to grocery shop or didn't have the money to buy food. Whenever she had access to food, she always overate. Earlier in the year she had gotten a horrible yearly physical—she was obese, prediabetic and her cholesterol was sky-high. That's when she decided to approach one of the personal trainers at the university's fitness center. Blake, who was the director of the personal training program at the university, rarely took on clients, but he had made time in his schedule for her as a favor for an old high school science partner.

"Hey, Isabella." Colt waved his hand.

The young girl had been watching the lights on the Christmas tree. She looked over at Colt.

"It was real nice meeting you. I bet I'll see you again real soon," Noah's brother said.

"Okay. 'Bye." Isabella gave him a little wave and then went back to watching the Christmas tree.

"I think you've created another Christmas monster," Noah mused.

"I was thinking the exact same thing," Shayna said as she stood up to give Colt a hug. "Give Lee my love."

Noah saw Colt to the door and hugged him goodbye.

"I've got your back, brother. But the clock is ticking," his brother reminded on his way out the door. "You know that."

"I do know it. All it takes is one person telling Mom that they've seen me in town," Noah acknowledged. "I just need a couple of more days, and then I'll get over to Sugar Creek."

"And you'll finally get to meet Junior in person."

"I'm looking forward to it." Noah gave his brother one last hug. "The Brand men are settling down."

"It will be your turn next," Colt said. "You should have been with Shayna from the get-go."

"Pull back on those reins, Colt. We're still just friends."

Colt sent him a disbelieving look. "Whatever you say, brother. I'll see you in a couple of days."

Noah closed the door behind him, still pondering Colt's out-of-the-blue comment about Shayna. Had marriage rattled his brain? Because his entire family damn well knew that Shayna had never been anything more than a friend. Now, he wasn't thrilled when heard that Blake Foreman was playing a big, unexpected part in Shayna's life. But that didn't mean anything. He'd never really liked sharing Shayna. For him, nothing had changed. She was his best friend, and that was all she was ever going to be.

"Hey!" he said. "Who's hungry?"

Isabella pried her attention away from the Christmas tree to look at him. "I am!"

"I think I could eat, too," Shayna said.

The moment Shayna looked into his face, they both said in unison, "Cosmic Pizza?"

Isabella bounced up and cartwheeled her way into the living room. "I want Cosmic Pizza, too!"

"Well, then. It's unanimous. Cosmic Pizza it is."

* * *

"I'm exhausted." Noah sat down heavily on the living room couch, put his arm on the back of the cushions and waited for her to join him.

They had filled up on pizza, worked together to tidy up some of the mess in the formal living room and then gotten Isabella cleaned up and put to bed.

"Me, too." Shayna sighed heavily, her head resting on the couch cushions, her eyes closed.

"Who would have thought that having a six-year-old could be so tiring?"

His companion turned her head toward him and opened her eyes to half-mast. "Literally everyone."

"Okay." He laughed. "Point taken."

Shayna closed her eyes again, and Noah found himself admiring her profile. Now that the shock of Isabella was fading a bit, Noah was beginning to notice all the little changes that his best friend had been making while he was overseas. She had straightened her teeth, returned to her natural honey-brown hair, grown her bangs out, and was now on a fitness journey. And even though he was happy for her in his own way, he had to acknowledge that the changes she was making made him feel uncomfortable and unsteady. Shayna had always been his rock, his harbor in any storm. That couldn't last forever, and he knew that. One day, some guy—maybe even Blake Foreman—would come along and steal Shayna's attention away from him.

"Ugh," Shayna groaned and patted her stomach. "I'm so stuffed I feel like I have a food baby in here."

"You only ate two pieces," Noah said disapprovingly. "The Shayna I used to know could eat an entire large pizza by herself."

Shayna sat up a bit with a frown. "That Shayna hasn't been around for a long time."

"I liked that Shayna," he said. "What kind of craziness has Foreman put in your head?"

His friend sat upright and faced him with a stormy look on her round face. "What is it that bothers you about Blake, Noah? Is it that someone actually enjoys my company?"

He shook his head, but she cut him off before he could say anything else.

"Just so you know, I really like Blake. He's a great guy and an amazing trainer." She pointed to her chest. "I'm lucky to have him in my life and, if we're as good friends as you've always said we are, then I would think that you would be happy for me. That you would *want* me to be healthy."

"I do." Noah quickly got two words in.

"I was on a road to dying young, Noah," she continued. "I had a horrible checkup with my doctor, and it finally snapped me into reality. So, *no*. I don't eat whole pizzas anymore. Not for you, not for anybody. I try my best to eat clean. I exercise. I choose me. You got that?"

"Okay." He sneaked another word in.

"You're upset because I've changed and that makes you uncomfortable?"

"I don't know that I said that, exactly." He tried to sneak in a quick defense. "I just always thought you were happy with who you were."

"Really? That's what you thought?"

He nodded, having the distinct feeling that he had just stepped on a land mine.

"You thought I enjoyed being fat?"

"You weren't fat."

She ignored him. "You thought that I liked being teased at school constantly and having kids make mooing sounds behind me? You thought that I enjoyed being the only girl in high school not to be asked to prom?"

"You said you didn't want to go."

"I lied!" Shayna snapped. "What else was I supposed to say? Of course I wanted to go! The only date I had that night was with Ben and Jerry. Okay? What was I supposed to say when people said to me, 'You have such a pretty face' but never finished the sentence—'if only you'd lose weight'? I was humiliated and mortified. The only thing I could do was to get really good at pretending that nothing people said mattered. But it did matter." There was sadness in her voice and unshed tears in her eyes when she said again, "It did matter."

"I always liked how you looked, Shay. I loved our marshmallow hugs." Noah had always loved to get a Shayna hug. Her body had been round and soft and somehow comforting to him. Now when he hugged her, her body felt more firm and strong. Not bad, really, just not the same.

Shayna stood up, her face flushed, her eyes darkened

to a stormy shade of forest green. "I love you, Noah. I really do. But sometimes you can be a real jerk."

"I don't mean to be." He was sitting with a straight back now, listening closely to Shayna's words.

She jabbed her finger in his direction. "For your information, Blake knows that I still want to have curves and that I'm not trying to achieve some magic number on the scale or some particular clothing size. I want to be healthy. I want my doctor to give me good news for a change. And if you really loved me, Noah, you would support me instead of giving me a hard time about how many pieces of pizza I eat."

Noah did the only thing he could think to do. He quickly got up off the couch and wrapped his arms around Shayna. At first, she resisted his hug, but with some patience on his part, she softened into his embrace.

He rested his chin on her head and said, "Hey. I *am* happy for you, Shay. Of course I am. I've just had a lot of crap dumped on me, and I guess it made me a bit stupid."

That blunt self-assessment had the impact Noah wanted—it made Shayna laugh.

"A bit?" Shayna asked playfully, and he was so grateful to have her teasing him.

"Okay." He leaned back so he could look down into her face. "Maybe more than a bit."

After they hugged a few seconds longer, Shayna

stepped away from him. He asked her sincerely, "Am I forgiven?"

"Yes," she said after a moment or two. "Aren't you always?"

"Thankfully, yes." He laughed. The last thing he wanted to do was alienate Shayna. Navigating instant fatherhood, jumping through legal hoops and finding a way to break the news to Isabella that he was her natural father was something he didn't want to do alone. When Shayna was by his side, he felt like he could do anything—*get through* anything.

Shayna yawned loudly and looked at the mess in the kitchen.

"Why don't you go on to bed and I'll take care of the kitchen." Noah rubbed her shoulders.

She made a happy noise, and he wasn't sure if it was the offer of cleaning up the kitchen or his massage.

"Are you serious, Captain Brand?"

"Of course."

Shayna said tiredly, "Are you trying to get on my good side again?"

"Always."

"Then I'll be happy to let you clean up the kitchen."

Shayna walked away from him, her long, wavy locks cascading down her back. In that moment, oddly, Noah wanted to pull her back into his arms, to have her close to him for a few minutes longer.

He was about to say something when her phone made a little chirp. Shayna looked at her cell and then typed something quickly before putting the phone back in her pocket.

"Anything important?" Noah asked, not really understanding himself why he felt so nosy about Shayna's personal life.

Shayna said, "That was Blake confirming our appointment for tomorrow."

"Tomorrow?"

"Yes, Noah." Her tone turned frosty again. "You can watch Isabella."

He must have looked absolutely petrified at the suggestion, because Shayna's expression softened when she said, "You'll be fine. You're great with her."

"That's because you were with us."

"No," Shayna replied. "You were great with her all on your own. It's time to put on your big-boy pants, Noah. You're a father now."

"That's what you keep telling me," Noah said, his tone a bit disgruntled and weary.

Shayna smiled at him with kindness in her tired eyes. "I keep telling you that because it's *true*. You will do fine without me. You'll see. You don't need me."

There was something in her voice—something in her eyes—that made him think that there was an undertone to her words. It was as if Shayna was preparing him for a time when it wasn't just *see you later* between them; it was as if she was preparing him for goodbye.

Noah stood in his place while he watched her disappear down the hallway with Pilot plodding along behind her.

"You're wrong this time, Shay. I do need you," Noah said quietly. He needed Shayna, and until that moment it hadn't fully occurred to him just how much he *did* need her.

After a really hard sleep, Shayna still felt groggy and fatigued from the stress of having a six-year-old and her best friend crash into her otherwise structured life. She almost called Blake to cancel but then thought better of it. After her declaration of independence the night before with Noah, she didn't want him to get the idea that she was changing her plans to please him.

She took a shower and rummaged through her new workout clothes to find something that she felt like wearing. Shayna took one last look at herself in the mirror; she smoothed her hands over her stomach, which was creating a noticeable bulge above her waistline. She did like her curves, but the potbelly was still a source of irritation.

She turned to the side and sucked in her stomach. After a few minutes, she breathed out quickly and gave up the attempt to hide the bulge. At least her breasts were still nice and plump and counterbalanced her problem area.

"Okay, Shayna." She took one last look in the mirror. "This is what we're working with. So just love it."

Shayna heard the doorbell ring, and she abandoned the mirror to rush out into the living room. She wanted to beat Noah to the front door, annoyed that he was still loitering around the house instead of taking Isabella to see May an hour ago like they'd planned. He should have already left, and Shayna was fully aware of the fact, unspoken or not, that Noah was lingering at the house so he could let Blake know that he was staying with her. Sometimes Noah was still a teenage boy; it used to not bother her so much, but lately, it was striking a nerve.

"Noah Brand." Blake had a ring of surprise in his voice. Blake was tall—taller than Noah—and he had a wonderful, Southern comfort, country smoothness in his deep baritone voice that was always pleasing to her ears.

"BB Gun." Noah didn't move out of his position in the doorway.

Blake smiled at the use of his old nickname. "No one's called me that in a long time."

The way the two men were standing reminded Shayna of two old fighters sizing each other up before they started whaling on each other.

"Hi, Blake!" Shayna scooted around Noah, brushing up against him in a way that made him move over a bit.

Blake, as always, had a kind smile for her. He was a handsome man with light brown hair, a dimple in his chin and a strong nose. Blake's golden-brown eyes were, in their own way, just as striking and memorable as Noah's blue ones. And his body—a body that had graced the cover of more than one fitness magazine— was totally noteworthy. Blake had on his usual tank top that showed off his thickly muscled biceps and sculpted shoulders, and he wore loose-fitting workout pants and tennis shoes. Blake looked completely at ease standing in her doorway. If Noah had hoped to rattle his old schoolmate, he hadn't succeeded.

"You ready?" her trainer asked her.

"Ready!" She smiled at him, glad now that she hadn't canceled. Blake always made her feel more energetic and capable. She loved that about him. To Noah she said, almost as an afterthought, "I'll see you later."

"Don't be too late," Noah said oddly.

"I won't, Dad," she teased Noah.

"I'll be sure to have her back before curfew." The trainer played along.

She walked next to Blake as they began their usual warm-up of walking her neighborhood. It was one of her favorite parts of her workout. They always had such interesting talks.

Just when she was about to lose sight of her front door, she looked over to find Noah still watching her, and she gave him a quick wave.

There was a small piece of her that almost felt sorry for Noah. He looked positively miserable that she was spending time with Blake.

"No," she said out loud when she meant to say it only in her mind.

"I'm sorry?" Blake asked as he kept pace with her.

Shayna gave a little wave of her hand. "I don't even know why I just said that."

But she did know. She was telling herself *no, I am not going to feel sorry for Noah*. His social media was filled with a merry-go-round of gorgeous women on the other side of the world. For once, she was stepping out with a handsome man while Noah was left behind with a wounded look on his face. And, honestly, she had to admit that it felt positively *wonderful*.

Chapter Five

"Thank you for coming to my house." Shayna had to work a bit harder to keep up with Blake's long stride. He always gave her a chance to warm up her legs before he lengthened his stride to get her heart pumping.

"I was glad to get your text. I was beginning to wonder if you'd given up."

"I haven't given up."

"I'm glad to hear it," Blake said sincerely. "How's the diet been?"

Ah, yes. The inevitable question had come sooner than she had hoped. The man certainly liked to get right to the point.

"Eh." She shrugged. "Hit or miss, honestly."

"Diet is ninety percent of the battle," her trainer reminded her for the umpteenth time.

"I know," she said with a sigh. "I know. It's just been a bit stressful lately."

"Life is always going to be stressful," Blake said matter-of-factly. "The key is to find new ways to cope with the stress other than eating."

"I know," she admitted. "You're right."

He looked over at her again with a kind expression. "I'm here to help you in any way I can. The next time you feel like you want to sabotage your diet, call me instead."

Shayna chuckled. "You don't really want me to do that, Blake. I get cravings in the wee hours of the morning."

"Anytime," he said. "Day or night."

She looked over at his strong profile. The man really was a catch—tall, handsome, great body and a kind heart. She knew he was single, but it was hard to believe that he didn't have his choice of companions. "Thank you, Blake. Seriously. You have no idea how much I appreciate your support on my journey to better health."

"That's what I'm here for." Blake lengthened his stride again. "When I have a client like you, someone who takes the advice and applies it, that's when I get really invested. You don't realize it, Shayna, but in my line of work, you're a rarity."

To get a compliment like that from a man who had dedicated his life to fitness and health gave her an unexpected boost of mental energy. She lengthened her own stride and pumped her arms to allow her to speed walk ahead of him. She glanced over her shoulder at him, smiled and said, "Pick up the pace a bit, slacker!"

"Slacker?" Blake laughed with a broad, genuine smile on his handsome face. That smile took Blake to the next level, from merely handsome to super hunk.

The trainer matched his pace to hers, and they both started to laugh when she pulled ahead again.

To be able to speed walk without losing her breath was exhilarating. Her mood felt light as a feather, and it put her in a teasing mood.

"You can do it, Blake." Shayna used one of Blake's favorite refrains when she was about to give up in the past. "Be the little engine that could."

"I think I can, I think I can." Always the good sport, Blake played along.

"I know you can." Shayna surprised even herself when she broke into a jog. "I know you can!"

By the time they tracked back to her driveway, her truck was gone, which meant that Noah and Isabella were gone, too. It was strange to her that she felt relieved, but she did.

"Do you want to go to the park or stay here?" Blake asked her.

They had stopped next to his large four-wheel-drive GMC truck.

Shayna was winded, and her skin was flushed from the walk. Yes, she was hot and sweaty and tired, but she was proud of herself for not letting Noah's drama with Annika derail her life. In the past, she would have dropped everything to rush to Noah's aid. This was the first moment when Shayna realized that she had changed. Her feelings for Noah *had* changed.

"Let's stay here," she said. "Do you mind?"

"Not at all." Blake opened the bed of his truck and pulled out a bin of equipment. "Gives me an opportunity to show you some quick and easy things you can do at home when you don't have much time."

"I'd like that."

Blake followed her inside the house, and they decided to set up in the backyard while Pilot lounged in the shade of a nearby tree. Even though she had missed several sessions with the sudden appearance of Isabella in her life, Blake didn't take it easy on her. He pushed her, as he always did, to do more than she'd ever thought she could. Blake's belief in her early on in her journey to health had allowed her to see herself in a different light and gave her the courage to transform into a person who cared about her health and put herself first after years of taking a back seat to the people in her life.

"Nice workout, Dr. Wade," Blake said as he bent over to return some of his weights to the bin.

Shayna was lying flat on her back in the grass, her chest rising and falling quickly, her body covered in sweat.

"I can't get up."

Blake snapped the lid of the bin before he came over to stand above her, his broad shoulders blocking the sun. He looked down at her in a way that made her feel a twinge of *something* that felt unfamiliar.

"Sure you can." Blake offered his hand to help her get up.

Her hand felt comfortable in his; Blake's hand was large, steady and strong, and the sight of his bicep tensing and bulging as he helped her to her feet was undeniably sexy.

"You know I silently curse you almost the whole entire time, don't you?" she asked him.

Blake laughed, a deep laugh that sent a shiver up her spine. "That means I'm doing my job."

Their eyes met, and Shayna felt a spark jump between them. And it was right then, in that moment, that she realized that she was capable of finding a man other than Noah attractive. It was a shocking but most welcome discovery.

Blake was a total hunk, and she was a single, red-blooded American female. Blake's transformation from the scrawny, picked-on kid at school into a fitness model who graced the covers of health magazines *and* turned the heads of many young college women whenever Shayna met him at the university gym to work out was appealing to her. And it wasn't just his outward appearance that attracted her—he was a sincere, kind man, too. Hot on the outside, a self-assured gentleman on the inside. A killer combo.

Shayna felt her body flush when Blake caught her contemplating him. He flashed that smile at her again, and darn it if her knees didn't get a little weak.

"Can I get you some water before you leave?" she said in a rush, trying to cover up her embarrassment at having been caught staring at him.

"Sure," Blake said easily.

Inside the house, Pilot made a beeline for his fluffy, comfy bed near the fireplace while Blake took a seat on one of her bar stools.

"Ice?"

"No, thanks," he said. "Straight up is fine."

"Here you go." She put a tall glass of water down in front of him.

Blake chugged the water before she could fill her own glass. She got him a refill and then leaned her hip against the counter while she quenched her thirst.

"You did good today," Blake said. "I'm proud of you."

"Thank you. I couldn't do it without you," she said and then asked, "More water?"

"Maybe just one more." He handed her the empty glass. "You're wrong, you know."

She filled up the glass to the rim and handed it back to him. "About what?"

"You were going to do this for yourself with or without me."

Shayna tilted her head to the side a bit, her arms crossed in front of her body. Sometimes Blake's willingness to connect with her on a deeper emotional level scared her.

"You've never doubted me," she said.

"Not for a second," her trainer said. "Even when we were kids, I knew how special you were."

"Thank you, Blake." Shayna felt a wave of emotion overwhelm her. His words struck a nerve. "I always felt pretty invisible back then."

"You weren't invisible to me." Blake said in his direct, cut-though-the-nonsense manner.

He chuckled for a second, his eyes focused on something behind her, as if he were remembering something funny.

"What?" she prodded him.

"I actually thought about asking you to prom."

Shayna froze in her spot, shocked at Blake's confession. Prom night had been a painful, lonely night for her. Her mom had been working the graveyard shift, and she was by herself. She remembered she had cried until her tears had soaked her pillow.

After a moment, a wrinkle in her brow, she asked, "Are you serious?"

He nodded, seeming more vulnerable in that moment than she had ever seen before. "You probably don't remember," Blake said, "but I tried a couple of times, and I just couldn't seem to get the words out of my mouth."

A memory, long forgotten until now, rose to the surface. "You stopped by my locker."

He nodded. "You had dropped your books."

"You were about to ask me something..." she remembered. "You said that you had something you wanted to ask me."

"And then—" Blake was channeling the same memory. Shayna didn't know if her expression matched the horrible feeling she had in her gut when she finished his thought. "And *then* Noah came up behind you, shoulder checked you..."

"And I lost my balance and face-planted on the floor."

Her hand went up to cover her mouth. That had been a horrible moment. Yes, Noah had helped Blake up and apologized, but the damage had already been done.

"I was so embarrassed—"

"I'm so sorry," she interjected.

"—that I never tried to ask you again."

They both were at a loss for words for several seconds. Shayna didn't believe that either had meant to go down this path and open up old wounds.

In her mind, Shayna saw the lanky, nerdy kid that Blake had been in high school standing before her. Yes, his outer shell had changed drastically, but just like her experiences in school had shaped her, so too had Blake's experiences shaped him. They both carried a lot of pain from being the oddball kids that never seemed to be able to fit in.

"I'm so sorry, Blake," she said again.

"It's ancient history."

She nodded her agreement, still a bit floored that she had almost had a date to prom. If Noah hadn't come along and bulldozed everything around him, how different would her life have been?

"I am curious," Blake said.

"About what?"

"Would you have said yes?"

"Yes," she said without a moment's hesitation. "I would have, yes."

"I knew I should've given it one more try." Blake caught her gaze and held it. "You can be sure I won't make that same mistake again."

Shayna had been caught off guard and thrown off balance by Blake several times the past hour. The way he was looking at her right now—as if he was appreciating the woman she had become—made her think that he was feeling the same attraction for her that she had been feeling for him.

Her arms automatically crossed in front of her body again. "I don't even know how we got onto this walk down horrible-memories lane."

Blake's gaze was direct when he said, "Seeing Noah brought back a lot of memories I had thought were long forgotten."

"I certainly understand that."

The trainer nodded his head, and then he paused before asking, "So, are you and Brand—?"

"No," she said quickly. "Still just friends."

Blake was about to say something when his phone chimed. He looked at the time. "I've got to get back to the gym."

"Of course," she said easily. "You've given me way more than the hour I pay for. I'll pay you the difference, I promise."

"No." Blake carried his bin of torture devices to the door. "That's on the house. I enjoy our time together."

"Me, too." She opened the door for him. "So, I'll see you next week?"

"I'll see you next week," Blake said, and of course, always the trainer, he said, "Make sure you send me your food journals for the week."

"Oh, boy." She laughed. "I can't wait to start journaling again."

Blake now had his serious trainer face on. "The research has shown that people who food journal have more success in losing weight than those who don't."

Shayna put her fist on her hip and looked at him as if she were hearing this information for the first time. "You don't say."

"Okay, okay." Blake flashed a grin. "I've said it to you a couple of times before."

"Just a couple," she joked with him. "You are persistent, Blake. That's what I love about you."

The words came out of her mouth, and she felt herself begin to blush, starting at her neck and racing upward to her face.

"Well, you know what I mean." She waved her hand as if to bat away the word *love* and the embarrassment that she felt.

"Don't worry." Blake did his best to put her at ease. "I knew what you meant."

"Okay." She laughed, still embarrassed. "Good."

"I'll look forward to seeing you next week, Shayna."

Shayna gave him one last wave and then shut the door. She leaned up against the door, looked up at the ceiling and tried to make sense of the last look Blake

Foreman had given her. It was different than any look he had ever given her before—more personal and somehow *intimate*. Was she imagining it, or was something developing between her and her trainer?

"He is handsome," Shayna said to Pilot, who had lifted his head when she closed the door. She walked over to give the old dog some love. "I wouldn't kick him out of my bed, that's for sure. You might." She dropped a kiss on Pilot's oversize head. "But I wouldn't."

"Nanna!"

The moment Isabella saw her grandmother propped up in the bed, she raced to her bedside and flung herself into May's arms. May had her arms open wide until the little girl reached her, and then she closed them tightly around Isabella's small frame.

"Oh, my sweetest baby girl," May said. "I've missed you so much."

"I want to go home, Nanna." Isabella held on just as tightly to her grandmother.

"I know you do, sweet-sweet." May kissed her granddaughter's head and petted her hair. "I know you do. So do I."

"Let's go now. I can take care of you."

"It's gonna be just a minute longer, baby girl. You just gotta be patient, and so do I."

May held out her hand for Noah to squeeze and mouthed the words *thank you*.

"Now, stand up and let me see your face."

Isabella stood upright but kept ahold of her grandmother's arm, as if she were afraid that May would disappear right before her eyes again.

"Look at you!" May exclaimed, her eyes full of love for the little girl. "You look like you growed a foot since I've seen you!"

"I don't think so." Isabella laughed and then collapsed onto May's chest again, her head resting on the woman's heart.

"Have you been a good girl for Mr. Noah and Miss Shayna?"

Isabella sneaked a quick glance in his direction. "Most of the time."

"That's good, baby girl." May laughed joylessly before she said to him, "Take a load off, Noah. You're hovering."

Noah sat down in the chair next to the bed.

"How are you feeling, May?" he asked.

"Right as rain." The older woman had a light in her eyes now that Isabella was with her. "They tell me I should be ready to go home in a week or two."

Isabella popped up in excitement. "That means I get to go home, too!"

May clasped the little girl's hand. "You betcha."

Noah didn't want to interrupt the reunion, and he certainly wasn't going to dampen the mood for Isabella, but he couldn't imagine how in the world May was going to look after a rambunctious, precocious six-year-old. Everything was way too muddy in his mind, and there wasn't much time—only a couple of weeks to figure out next steps for his daughter. Even without a DNA test, he was convinced that Isabella was his child, and he needed to have some say in what happened to her. That was his right as her father. Surely May had to agree with that—things couldn't just return to the way they had been before he knew that Isabella existed in the world.

Noah sat back and watched Isabella with her grandmother. The bond was unmistakable. Isabella had been only three when her mother left her with May so she could chase after Millburn. Of course, she would latch on to the only person who had given her constant love and attention. Noah couldn't even imagine how to navigate all the challenges before all of them.

"This is Shayna's carousel." Isabella had found her way beside May on the bed and the two of them were scrolling through pictures of Shayna's Christmas collection on his phone.

"Isn't that something?" May brushed Isabella's hair off her face affectionately. "You know, I spent a lot of time with Shayna when she was your age."

"You did?" Isabella asked.

"Sure I did," May said. "She lived right across the street from me, and she used to come over for dinner."

"Was she friends with my mom?"

May paused in thought. "I know they liked each other."

A cloud passed over Isabella's pretty, impish face. "I miss Mom."

Her grandmother's face crumpled as she wrapped the little girl into her arms. "I know you do, sweet-sweet. I do, too. But as soon as she's done with everything she has to do, I know she'll come right home in a flash."

May met his gaze over the top of Isabella's head. It was a lie—they both knew it—but it was a lie to help a child cope with her mother's abandonment. It had to be done.

"If I help Shayna put up her Christmas display, I bet Mom will come to see it."

May hugged her even tighter. "Of course she will, my love. Of course she will."

Seeming satisfied with the idea that the Christmas display would magically make Annika appear back in Bozeman, Isabella showed May all the photos of Shayna's house, including tons of pictures of Pilot.

"We should be heading back home." He held his hand out for his phone. "Pilot needs to be fed, and we need to figure out what we're going to do for dinner."

Isabella frowned at him and then sank more deeply into her spot next to May. "Why don't I stay here with Nanna and you go?"

May smiled and kissed her granddaughter on the top of her dark head. "I wish you could. But they only let old bags like me stay here. In the meantime, take lots of pictures for our next visit. Okay?"

"Okay," Isabella said, disappointed.

May kissed her granddaughter again and then patted her on the arm to signal that she should get down off the bed. Isabella was much more obedient with May, Noah noticed; his daughter followed the gentle but firm command of her grandmother and climbed down off the bed.

"Noah," May said, her voice weakened from all the talking and excitement of the visit. "Open that drawer right there."

Noah slid open the drawer next to the bed.

"There's a piece of paper in there. Do you see it?"

He saw a folded piece of note paper, lifted it up and showed May. "This?"

She nodded. "Put that in your pocket. I've had some news."

Noah unfolded the piece of paper and saw an address in Colorado scrawled in May's shaky handwriting. Wordlessly, he put the paper in his pocket as instructed. He caught May's eye—she had found out where Annika was staying, and the thought of finding his childhood sweetheart made his heart race in a way that frustrated him.

Noah leaned over and kissed May on the cheek. "Thank you, May."

"No." The woman's eyes were damp with emotion as she reached for his hand. "Thank you, Noah. May God bless you always."

The next day, Noah awakened with a renewed sense of purpose. For the first couple of days back in Bozeman, he had still been processing the shock of Isabella. Now, the shock had worn off, and he needed to act. He was out of bed before dawn, he got in a run and then he showered, shaved and borrowed Shayna's old truck that she had been driving around since high school because it was less conspicuous than the Chevelle.

"Where have you been?"

Shayna was sitting on the ground with a sketch pad on her lap and her reading glasses perched on the bridge of her nose; Isabella was sitting close to her, her hair falling in a long, thick braid down her back.

Noah sat down on the nearby couch. "I went to see an old friend."

"We figuring out where all of the princesses are going to go," Isabella informed him in a very serious manner.

"If that's the case, where are you going to be?" he asked his daughter. Day by day, when he said the word *daughter* in his head, it sounded less foreign.

Isabella appeared perplexed for a moment, her blue eyes—his own eyes—looking back at him. And then her smile, such a quirky, cute, smile, began to appear when she realized that he was acknowledging her princessness. Noah found himself very enamored with that smile; he could see himself working day after day to create more smiles, just like that one, on his daughter's face.

"I don't know," Isabella said seriously. Then she turned to Shayna. "Where am I going to go?"

Shayna, ever the angel in his life, scanned the rough sketch of her Christmas display. "I don't know. Where do you think Princess Isabella should go?"

Isabella got up onto her knees so she could better scan the sketch. After a moment, Isabella gingerly touched the sketch with her pointer finger.

"I should go right there."

"All right." Shayna flipped to an empty page in her sketchbook. "Let's see what Princess Isabella looks like." Noah watched as Shayna put her considerable artistic skills to use in a sketch of Princess Isabella.

Chapter Six

As seriously as an artist would address a paying client with deep pockets, Shayna asked Isabella, "What kind of dress do you want your princess to wear?"

"Purple with a really big skirt."

Shayna quickly drew the body of the princess with a sweetheart neckline and an enormous hoopskirt with flower pickups. The princess had Isabella's face—Shayna, without much effort, had created an incredible likeness of his daughter.

"Something like this?" She showed the sketch to Isabella.

His daughter's pretty face was alight with joy, and her eyes widened in amazement. "It's me!"

"Of course, Princess Isabella," Shayna said affectionately. "Now for the best part." Shayna opened her tackle box filled with rows of perfectly sharpened colored pencils. "What shade of purple should we use for your dress?"

Isabella had a very serious, intent look on her face, and she bit her lip while she thoughtfully scanned all the pencils. Biting his lip when he was thinking or focusing on a project was something that he did all the time—had done since he was a kid.

Finally, Isabella selected a dark shade of purple. "This one."

"Nice choice." Shayna pulled the pencil out of its spot and read the name of the shade. "Well, this was just meant to be."

She held up the pencil for Isabella to read. "You picked Plum Princess."

"Plum Princess," Isabella repeated with wonder in a way only a young girl could muster.

Shayna's hands worked quickly, and in no time at all the dress came to life in the shade of purple Isabella had chosen. After the dress was complete, Shayna wrote in loopy, fancy cursive at the top of the sketch, Isabella the Plum Princess.

"Wow." Isabella stared at her likeness in awe.

"Do you like it?" Shayna prodded.

Isabella nodded and, without warning, hugged Shayna quickly. Stunned, Shayna caught Noah's eye over the little girl's head. The look on her friend's face was priceless—a mixture of shock and happiness.

"You're welcome, Isabella," Shayna said.

"I'm going to take Pilot outside with me." Isabella broke the hug and jumped down off the chair.

"Okay," Shayna replied. "Bring him back in if he gets too hot."

"I will," Isabella promised.

Shayna stood up, sketchbook in hand.

"May I?" He held out his hand.

"Of course." Shayna handed him the sketchbook.

Noah examined the sketch of his daughter as the Plum Princess. "My God, Shay. Your talent never ceases to amaze me."

"Thank you." His friend leaned back on the couch. Quietly, she said, "You do know that if you keep on visiting old friends, your secret isn't going to be much of a secret anymore."

"I called Mom this morning." He put the sketchbook on the coffee table. "Let her know I'm in town."

Shayna twisted her long hair into a knot on top of her head. "Did you? How did that go?"

"She's excited I'm in town," he said. "And curious."

"So, you didn't tell her."

"That's news better left for in person."

"True."

"I'm going out to Sugar Creek this afternoon."

"Good." Shayna looked relieved. "That's good."

"I'm thinking about taking Isabella with me."

"No. That's not a good idea, Noah."

"Mom's going to want to meet her the second I tell her."

"Of course she will. But—"

"I know what you're thinking, Shay. But you haven't seen May in person. She looks really weak and shaky. I'm on a time crunch, and things aren't going to be ideal, that much I know. If May can't take her back to live with her—and by the looks of things, I would say that's an unlikely scenario, especially once Isabella goes back to school—Mom might have to step in when I go back overseas."

Shayna absorbed his words. "It's all happening so fast."

"I know. I wasn't expecting to be an instant father."

"No," his friend said pensively. "It's going to take much longer than we have to make sense of all of this. And we're adults. I can't imagine how tough this is all going to be for Isabella."

"I have been thinking the same thing. That's why I really need my family on board on this." Noah reached out and took Shayna's hand in his. "I really want you to come out to Sugar Creek with us. You could show Isabella the barn while I go speak with Mom. Dad's at a farm equipment sale in Boise with Bruce, so there will be fewer Brands milling about."

Shayna was glad to hear that Jock and the oldest Brand boy, Bruce, were out of town. They both could be pretty stubborn, traditional and inflexible. They weren't going to be happy to find out that the Annika saga was not over.

"Come on, Shayna." He smiled at her gently. "I need you."

They stared at each other for several seconds before

she gave the faintest of nods. "Okay. If you think that's what's best."

"I do."

They both stood up and naturally walked over to the bay window to check on Isabella. Of course, she was lying down in the grass talking animatedly to Pilot, who was happy to be her pillow.

"Who was the old friend?" Shayna asked, her eyes still on Isabella.

Noah joined her at the window. "I went to see Judge Silvernail."

Judge Silvernail was a longtime friend of the family—he had overseen an adoption for Noah's older brother Liam, and he had sentenced Colt to community service at a therapeutic riding facility owned and operated by Colt's future wife, Lee. Now, once again, Judge Silvernail was coming to the aid of the Brand family by helping Noah to establish paternity.

"And?"

"He recommended a lawyer," Noah shared. "I need to file an emergency petition with the court to establish paternity. I've got to get this done before I leave."

"I can't imagine that May will be thrilled with any of this."

"Maybe not. But she had to know that things were going to change when she tracked me down."

There was a pregnant pause that made Shayna look over at her friend. "What else?"

"There's this." He pulled a piece of paper out of his wallet and handed it to her. Now the mystery of Annika's whereabouts was solved; Annika had called May from a substance abuse rehabilitation facility in Oregon.

Shayna unfolded it; Noah watched her face very closely. Shayna looked at the writing for a very long time before she folded the paper slowly and handed it back to him. The warm, rosy tone of her cheeks had blanched white, and he knew that the thought of Annika returning to their lives brought up many feelings for Shayna. It had for him.

"When are you going to reach out to her?" There was an emotional waver in her voice that she tried to hide, but she couldn't keep that sort of thing from him. And that worked both ways in their relationship.

"Soon," he said. "I need to confirm paternity first. So I can confront her with the facts—I wouldn't put it past her to lie and deny."

Shayna had taken a tiny step away from him. He noticed it, but he didn't mention it; her arms were crossed protectively in front of her body. Noah did recognize that his messy relationship with Annika was bringing unwanted drama into Shayna's life.

"And what about Isabella?" she asked, still staring straight ahead. "When are you going to tell her? *How* are you going to tell her?"

"I don't have a clue, Shay. I don't think it makes sense to destroy the fairy tale that her mother wove about Millburn and then go back overseas."

"Why don't you make an appointment with Dr. Friend? I went to see her for a while when I was trying to figure out why I was always sabotaging my path to a healthier life."

Dr. Friend, a local psychologist, had helped his brother Bruce and Savannah repair their marriage after the loss of their son.

"I'll do that."

Wanting to see a smile on Shayna's face—to see the cute dimple in her left cheek show—Noah reached out and pulled her hair out of the bun. and the caramel and gold wavy locks fell down her back. Noah caught the scent of honeysuckle from Shayna's freshly washed hair. For a split second, he had to resist the impulse to bury his nose in her neck and inhale her sweet smell.

As he had hoped, Shayna smiled at him and allowed him to pull her into a side hug. With her next to him, his arm resting on her shoulders, Noah watched his daughter executing perfect handstands in the yard.

"I feel like I'm sleepwalking through a dream. I still can't believe that she exists and that she's mine."

"I'm in the same boat," she agreed. "So surreal. Like looking at a Salvador Dalí painting." Shayna continued in a soft voice, "Whatever I can do to make all of this easier on her, I'll do."

"I know you will. That's why I love you so much." Noah kissed Shayna on the head, his heart so full of love for her. Of course, Annika was the one who'd created this mess, and of course it was Shayna who was there, always there, to help him clean it up.

"You do know that I love you, don't you, Shay?" he said.

She grabbed the hand resting on her shoulder and squeezed it. "Of course I do, Noah. And I love you. Friends for life."

When Shayna said "friends for life," something hit him wrong in the gut. He knew that he had solid competition in Blake Foreman—he had seen the way the other man looked at Shayna. Maybe it was time for him to knock out the competition with one blow and explore that "something more" that was always just below the surface of their decades-long friendship. Just maybe it was well past time.

It had been years since Shayna had gone to Sugar Creek Ranch. The Brand family owned a huge cattle spread outside Bozeman, and most of Noah's six older siblings worked the land. Jock Brand, the patriarch and founder of Sugar Creek, had been married twice and fathered a total of eight children. Bruce, the eldest, lived on Sugar Creek land with his wife, Savannah, and their spunky redheaded daughter. Most of the family believed that Bruce would inherit the bulk of Sugar Creek when Jock died. Liam, the second oldest, was a large-animal vet who was married to a horse trainer, Kate King Brand. Liam and his wife had built their dream home on Kate's family land with Kate's only child, Calico, an adult living with Down syndrome. Calico was engaged and, last Shayna had heard, she was planning for a June wedding the following year.

"There's Gabe's place," Shayna mused aloud as they

passed the entrance to Little Sugar Creek. "Is he out on the road?"

"Gabe's a rolling stone." Noah glanced over at his older brother's property. "He's lucky Bonnie's got her own thing or their marriage would've tanked a long time ago."

Gabe was a long-distance horse hauler for the rich and famous, and that job was how he'd met his beautiful wife, Bonita De La Fuente. Gabe had hauled Bonnie's show horse from Washington, DC, to Montana, and even though the two of them were polar opposites, love was more powerful than their differences. After Bonnie had graduated with her medical degree, and once her residency was over, she had moved to Bozeman and opened a private practice.

Noah's three other older brothers—Shane, Hunter, and Colt, were all married. The only unmarried Brand siblings were Noah and the youngest, a girl, Jessie. And Shayna knew full well that if Annika hadn't flaked out on Noah that he would have married her. The Brand men were the marrying kind.

Noah slowed to turn onto the long, winding, bumpy dirt road that led to the enormous farmhouse that Jock had built to show off his wealth.

"I want a horse," Isabella said from the back seat. "Even since I was little."

"Ever since you were little?" Noah looked in the rearview mirror.

Isabella nodded definitively. "Dad promised me a

horse as soon as he gets back from his trip. He can't call me because he's in the mountains."

Shayna saw Noah's knuckles tighten on the steering wheel until they were blanched white.

"Well, you'll have plenty of horses to meet here." Shayna craned her neck to the left so she could look at Isabella. "Sugar Creek has hundreds of horses."

"Hundreds?" Isabella asked.

Noah's fingers loosened their grip a bit. "Hundreds."

"Whoa."

Shayna laughed along with Noah. "Totally whoa."

The Brand holdings were vast, with hundreds of acres of pastures ripe for grazing cattle, streams that she had fished in when she was a kid and several ponds where Noah had taught her how to float on her back. Sugar Creek had been, for so many years, the center of her universe, and it was a place, much like May's house, where she had always felt accepted and safe.

Noah pulled up to one of the many barns situated away from the main house. "I'll let the two of you spend some time with the horses while I head up to the main house."

"Come on, Isabella. This is our stop," Shayna said.

She didn't have to ask the little girl twice—Isabella had unbuckled her seat belt, thrown open the back door to Shayna's truck and jumped down to the ground.

"Come on, Shayna!" Isabella held her arms out wide from her body, her fingers tensed with anticipation. "Hurry!"

"You'll be okay?" Noah asked her as she stepped out of the truck.

She had plenty of experience with horses. She wasn't the best rider, but she felt confident in her skills when on the ground.

"Go handle your business." She shut the passenger door behind her. "I've got this."

"Noah!" Lilly Brand exclaimed when she saw him.

Noah had found his mother in her greenhouse next to the farmhouse. Noah knew that Lilly hadn't wanted the massive house Jock had built for her, so this greenhouse, along with her sewing and craft room, were the two places Lilly called her own.

"My son." His mother grabbed his face and kissed him on both cheeks before she hugged him tightly. "My beautiful son."

"I'm glad to see you, *ninga*." Noah used the Ojibwe word for *my mother* when he returned his mother's embrace. Until that moment, he hadn't realized just how much he had missed her.

Lilly was a full-blooded Chippewa Cree Native American, while his father, Jock, was Scottish. From Lilly, he had inherited his dark hair and golden-hued skin; from his father, the prominent, straight nose and his deep-set blue eyes.

"Come. Sit." Lilly took him by the hand, holding on to it as if she were afraid that if she let go he would disappear.

She led him to a nearby two-seater white table, and

together they sat. His mother's straight black hair was more silver than he remembered and the lines around her black-brown eyes more deep, but her beauty, even as she aged, was undeniable, as were her calm nature and wide-open heart. His mother was a spiritual woman in touch with nature and reverent of the tribal ancestors.

Still holding on to his hand, his mother asked, "Why are you home, son?"

"Something's come up."

"Yes." Lilly studied him with an expectant eye. "It must have. Don't use many words when a few will get the job done."

Noah nodded, remembering that his mother liked her information straight, no chaser. "I have a daughter."

It was a rare moment when Lilly was moved to silence. She was quiet for several moments, processing his words. Finally, she said, "A daughter."

He nodded as he covered her hand, still holding his, with his free hand. "Her name is Isabella May."

Lilly's face turned ashen. "Annika's daughter."

Noah leaned in a bit. "You know about her?"

"I've met her. Just once. At the grocery store." Tears began to well up in Lilly's eyes, and she put her free hand over her quivering lips. "I thought there was something so familiar about the little girl—and Annika was acting so strangely."

Noah reached up and gently wiped the tears from his mother's cheeks with his fingers. "Don't cry, *ninga*."

"I am not crying for myself, my son. The universe

wanted me to meet my grandchild, and so I did. I am crying for you."

Noah felt rage bubble up from his gut; he had to swallow back the bile and try to keep calm for his mother's sake. But Annika had introduced Lilly to her own granddaughter without letting on, for one second, that Isabella was Lilly's own flesh and blood! He was already having a difficult time figuring out how to forgive his ex-fiancée for what she had done to him. To do that to his mother was another thing entirely. Lilly didn't deserve anyone's cruelty.

"Don't cry for me. I have a beautiful daughter." Noah slid his hands free and took his phone out of his back pocket. He went to his pictures, found one he had taken of Isabella with Pilot in the backyard of Shayna's house and showed it to his mother.

Wordlessly, Lilly took the phone in one hand, and her other hand went to rest on her cheek. His mother made a sound in the back of her throat—an odd sound that was filled with both sorrow and joy—and then the tears began to fall from her eyes again, but she wouldn't let him dry them a second time.

"These are tears of joy, and I want to feel them for a moment longer on my skin. She is so beautiful," Lilly said. "Just like you."

He couldn't disagree. He had made a beautiful child with Annika—she was smart, pretty and so full of potential. Yet, for one so young, she was too adult by far. Thanks to her mother and Jasper, Isabella had had to deal with things beyond her years—she had been forced to grow up way too fast.

"And where is the child now?" his mother asked, handing the phone back to him.

"At the barn."

Lilly's eyebrows lifted. "Which barn?"

"The red barn."

His mother stood up and dried her own tears. "Take me to my grandchild."

On the short drive to the red barn, Noah quickly explained the circumstances and his plan to ensure that he was recognized as Isabella's legal father.

"She doesn't know," Noah reminded his mother. "Not yet."

"Son." Lilly put her steady hand on his arm. "Don't let worry poison your mind."

As they always did, his mother's simple words of advice calmed him down when he was overthinking a problem. He took a deep breath in and let it out as he parked Shayna's truck in front of the small red barn.

With one final squeeze of his arm, Lilly said, "Be respectful to the Creator and life, Noah. Our largest blessings often come wrapped in our most difficult adversity."

Noah stared at his mother, who often talked in philosophical terms. "Remember, she doesn't know that I'm her father. She doesn't know that you are her grandmother."

Lilly smiled broadly at him, the creases around her eyes abundant and deep, and gave his arm one final squeeze—to, he assumed, reassure him that his secret was safe with her. "Don't let worry poison your mind."

Together they walked with purpose into the barn, their feet leaving prints in the sandy aisle.

"You have always leaned too heavily on Shayna Wade," Lilly said quietly for only him to hear.

"She's my best friend."

Lilly looked up at him. "She is the kind of woman any mother would love to have as a daughter-in-law. If you can't do right by her, Noah, it is time for you to let her go."

Noah was still mulling over his mother's pointed comment about Shayna. Of course, the entire Brand clan loved Shayna—as did he! That's why he couldn't figure out what his mother had meant by letting Shayna go. Noah wanted to ask his mother what she had meant by her unnecessary defense of Shayna's honor, but Lilly was singularly focused on her granddaughter.

"I see you've found Wildflower," Lilly said in her sweet, lilting voice.

"We gave her a couple of treats from the tack room. I hope that was okay." Shayna gave Lilly a strong, quick hug. "It's wonderful to see you again, Mrs. Brand."

"It's long past time for you to call me Lilly," his mother said. "And it's wonderful to see you again, too, Shayna."

"Thank you… Lilly." His friend hesitated for a moment before she shyly used his mother's given name for the first time.

Lilly put her hand on Shayna's upper arm affectionately and asked, "And who is this?"

Isabella was too enamored with the petite, dappled gray mare named Wildflower to pay much mind to anything or anyone else.

"Mom, this is Isabella, May's granddaughter."

"Hello, Isabella." Lilly extended her hand to the girl. "What a pretty girl you are."

"Hi." His daughter gave her grandmother a quick shake of the hand, hardly looking at her. "Is this your horse?"

"Yes, she is," Lilly said, seemingly unaffected by the little girl's singular focus on the horse. "Do you like her?"

"Oh, yes." Isabella nodded. "I do."

While Shayna stepped back with him, Lilly stepped forward and put her hand gently on the mare's dappled gray-and-blue neck. Wildflower had a muscular body and a thick, shaggy black mane and tail that were a lovely contrast to her gray-blue dappled body and the four black socks on her legs. Her face was steel gray with a black muzzle and not a speck of white on the forehead.

"She was a gift from my husband," Lilly told Isabella. "She's a mustang. When I got her, she was so wild I couldn't touch her. But now she's as gentle as a butterfly. I can ride her bareback anywhere with just a halter and a lead rope."

Isabella looked up at Lilly with hopeful eyes. "Can I ride her?"

"Have you ever ridden before?"

His daughter nodded. "Once. At Granny Millburn's house."

Noah's eyes shot over to his mother at the mention of Millburn's mother, who'd had the privilege of being Isabella's grandmother for the first six years of her life. Still, Lilly hadn't missed a beat. But, then again, that was his mother. She would not get hung up on the past but would accept the present and trust that everything had unfolded exactly how it was supposed to unfold. Oh, how he wished he had his mother's unwavering faith in the universe.

Chapter Seven

"What do you think, Wildflower?" Lilly asked the horse seriously. "Would you be willing to give Isabella a ride today?"

Noah took a step forward to interject his opinion, but Shayna put her hand on his arm to stop him.

Wildflower ducked her dainty head to nibble on Lilly's shirt. "Wildflower would like to give you a ride."

His daughter's face lit up, her blue eyes wide and bright with excitement.

"Mom." He didn't share the enthusiasm. "Do you think that's really a good idea?"

Lilly gave him a calm look. "Son, go fetch the hoof pick and pick out Wildflower's hooves. Your hands need something to do."

Noah did what he was told, knowing that he was outnumbered. Lilly spoke in quiet tones to the horse in Ojibwe, a language he wished he had learned when he was a boy. Lilly showed Isabella how to brush Wildflower's coat, mane and tail. Noah noticed that his daughter was completely focused on his mother now, seeming to want to soak up everything she could learn about the pretty little mare. May was right—at times, Isabella seemed much older than her chronological age.

"Watch how she puts her nose into the halter. She wants to help me." Lilly showed Isabella how to put the halter on the mustang.

Lilly led the mare out of the stall and into an adjacent riding arena, which had been overgrown in the middle with weeds.

"I need to cut those weeds down," Noah noted.

"I believe so," his mother agreed. "Lift her on to Wildflower's back, Noah."

Noah had the privilege—and he did feel that it was a privilege—of lifting up his daughter and placing her carefully on Wildflower's back.

"Now, go ahead and hook your finger around a piece of her mane—don't pull on it, just hold on to keep your balance."

Isabella followed the direction and then, as Lilly directed, squeezed her legs to ask Wildflower to walk forward. The joy on Isabella's face was contagious as Lilly led the mare around the arena.

On the other side of the ring, Isabella waved one of her arms in the air. "Look at me!"

"We see you!" Shayna called out. "You're doing great!"

"You know what you are?" Noah called out to his daughter.

"What?" Isabella asked loudly enough for him to hear.

"A real, live cowgirl."

To his mind, he had spoken the absolute truth. Isabella had a natural seat on a horse. With some lessons, Noah had no doubt that Isabella would grow into a talented horsewoman just like his sister and his mother. And one day he was going to make sure that his daughter got her wish. One day Isabella was going to have her very own horse kept right here on Sugar Creek Ranch.

The day she had spent on Sugar Creek Ranch with Noah and Isabella had been a magical day for Shayna. It had brought back so many fond memories of her formative years that it had been nearly impossible to stop those memories from flooding her mind for the next few days. Isabella appeared to fit right in on the ranch, and Lilly, of course, was such an amazingly kind woman who had made her feel like no time at all had passed since the last time Shayna had been to the ranch.

Shayna had just finalized her drawing for her Christmas wonderland princess display and was flipping through the pictures of Isabella and Noah at the ranch. This was something she did several times a day, loving the happiness she saw so clearly on Noah's face when he was interacting with his daughter. And she had to admit that in the pictures of her with Isabella and Noah that Lilly had taken, she looked happy as well. They made a handsome family, Isabella, Noah and her. It was dangerous for her to even be entertaining the thought that she could be a family with Noah and Isabella. It was a fool's folly, and yet she couldn't stop herself from fantasizing.

The phone rang and startled her out of her dream weaving. It was Blake.

"Hi, Blake," she said with a genuine smile in her voice. The man had perfect timing. She'd needed something to jar her out of her own thoughts.

"Hi, Shayna," her trainer said with a fondness in his tone for her.

There was a pause, and then it clicked in her mind. "Oh, shoot! My food journal! I promised to get it to you and I forgot. And that's not an excuse. I promise. I really have been doing it! The minute we get off the phone, I'll take some pics and text them to you."

Another pause.

"Blake?" She sat back in her chair. "Are you still there?"

She looked at her phone to make sure that they were still connected.

"Actually, I wasn't calling about the food journal," he finally said. "But I am glad that you are keeping one."

"It's been a pain, but it's helped. I went down a pant size—that hasn't happened in years."

"Do you feel better? Have more energy?"

"I do," Shayna said. "I can't believe that I would ever

say this, but I'm looking forward to seeing my doctor in a few months. I think my lab work will be much better next time."

Another odd pause on the line made her wrinkle her forehead curiously. "Well, I guess I'd better let you go, Blake. I'll see you next week."

"Hold on."

She waited.

"Like I said, I wasn't calling about the food journal."

Her curiosity piqued, Shayna waited for his next words.

"I actually called to ask you if you wanted to go out to dinner with me."

Shayna had been doodling on the edge of her Christmas display plan, making little hearts; when Blake asked her out on a date, her fingers froze. And so did her mouth. She couldn't get one word to come out.

"Shayna?" Now he was asking if she was still on the line. This was the most awkward conversation she had ever had with Blake.

"I'm here."

"And?" he prodded.

Did she want to go out to dinner with Blake? After a moment or two of thought—and the realization that a date with Blake, a handsome, available man, would be a wonderful way to counteract the recent bout of fantasizing about Noah—Shayna said, "Yes. I'd like to go out with you to dinner Blake, with two conditions."

"Which are?"

"It's on my cheat day *and* you don't give me any grief about what I eat. Not a look, not a peep!"

"Done. What's the other condition?"

"That you will still be my trainer no matter what."

"Scout's honor," he said solemnly. "That will not change."

"Were you a scout?" she asked.

"Absolutely, I was," he said. "I made it all the way to Eagle Scout."

"But of course you did." She laughed, and he laughed along with her. It was, for the most part, so easy to talk to Blake. He was straightforward, uncomplicated, and they always made each other laugh.

The more his invitation to dinner sank in, the more Shayna began to feel excited about it. They made plans for him to pick her up at her house the following evening, and when Shayna hung up the phone, it hit her that, for the first time in her life, she wanted to keep the date a secret from Noah.

"The date." Shayna stood up and twirled around like a teenage girl. She hadn't been out on a date in such a long time. The COVID pandemic had completely cramped her dating life—not that it was robust before the country went on lockdown and masked up. She had been quite lonely teaching virtually from home; this loneliness was what had inspired her to seek out the company of a geriatric Great Dane.

"Holy cow," she said to Pilot, who didn't bother to wake up at the news. "I was right. There *is* something between us."

Shayna hadn't bothered to ask Blake where this left them in the trainer-client relationship. Blake was handsome and kind and incredibly smart—if she had to give him up as her trainer to explore a possible romantic connection, then she was perfectly willing to do it. And, from the evidence of him asking her out on a date, he was like-minded.

"Why so happy?" Noah walked into the room trailed by Isabella. They had been away from the house for several hours visiting May and running errands.

Not wanting to give Noah a chance to spoil the happiness she was feeling, she said, truthfully, "I finished the sketch."

Noah and Isabella both admired the finalized sketch, and Isabella was particularly pleased with the placement of the Plum Princess by the sidewalk. Isabella's alter ego, the Plum Princess, would be the first and most prominent character in the display. Front and center.

"What's next?" Noah asked her, and he seemed genuinely interested in her process.

Shayna ran her hand over the sketch to smooth out any wrinkles in the paper. "A materials list and checking all of the lights that I have in my stockpile already."

"I can help with that," Isabella said.

"I'd like that." She smiled at the little girl who reminded her so much of herself at that age—so eager to be helpful and a part of something bigger than herself.

"What about the village?"

Shayna looked around at the scattered parts of the village. She had unpacked them to show Isabella, and now they were making a cluttered mess in the formal living room.

"I suppose I should fast-track that project."

"I'm pretty handy with a nail gun and a saw," Noah reminded her.

She smiled at him. "I remember."

Noah looked around the main living room. "I think I could install the continuous shelves that you want for the display before I go."

Shayna gave her friend a spontaneous hug and kissed him affectionately on the cheek. "I knew I was friends with you for a reason, Noah."

Noah held her tight against his body, lingering in the hug. "Friends with benefits."

His flirtation didn't faze her—he had done that for most of their friendship and she had finally, for the most part, learned to ignore it. For years, her heart used to flutter wildly whenever he flirted with her. But she was older now—wiser—and she had learned to protect the romantic part of her heart from Noah Brand.

She gave his chest a pat, signaling the end of the hug, and she passed on the opportunity to flirt with him. Back in the day, she would have lived hopefully on the word *benefits* for months. Her relationship with Noah had always been so complicated for her—on one hand, she was immune to his flirting; on the other hand, not even thirty minutes ago she had been dreaming about what it would be like to be Isabella's bonus mom.

Lord—she really did need that date with Blake!

"Well," she said easily, "if you build my shelf for me, there isn't a better benefit you could offer me."

It was a flippant comment, one that was intended to stop the flirting and make Noah laugh. And he did laugh. But she knew him well enough to know that there was a split second of pain in his eyes. The man certainly loved to keep her off balance; it was up to her to keep herself upright and moving forward.

"Shayna. Are you in there?" Noah knocked on her bedroom door. He had just gotten off the phone with his attorney, and the first person he wanted to discuss the results of the meeting with, as always, was Shayna. Isabella was spending the day with his mother at Sugar Creek. The entire family had been informed about his daughter with Annika, but, unusually, everyone was showing restraint for Isabella's sake.

"Come on in," she called out to him.

When he opened the door, thinking that he would suggest that they order in and discuss his case, he was greeted with a moist heat in the room from a recent shower and the notes of white grapefruit and sandalwood, a hallmark of Shayna's special-occasion perfume. Shayna came out of the bathroom dressed in a figure-hugging black wrap dress and strappy high heels. Her curvy legs were bare, and she was wearing her standard toe ring and a dainty ankle bracelet. Her toes were painted a ruby red. The front of the dress was a V-neck that emphasized her cleavage. Shayna had developed young and had always been big busted. This was the first time he could remember truly noticing her chest the way a man notices that sort of thing on an attractive woman. The working out with Foreman had changed her body—her waist was defined and her muscles taut. Her figure was curvy and voluptuous, like Hollywood actresses or pinup girls in the 1950s.

"You look—" He stopped himself from saying *beautiful*, even though he did think she looked absolutely beautiful. And, if he were being completely honest, she also looked sexy. "Nice."

She had applied her makeup with a light hand, and her long, wavy hair was shiny and loose.

"Thank you." She gave him a pleased, self-conscious smile.

"You're going out?" He could hear the surprise in his voice.

It was then that Noah noticed Shayna definitely appeared to be a bit sheepish. She lowered her eyes for a moment before she lifted her chin with a shy smile and said, "Actually, yes. I have a date."

Noah couldn't explain it, but his knees nearly buckled right out from beneath him. He had to lock his legs to stop himself from falling over.

"BB Gun finally got the nerve up to ask you out, did he?" He sounded bitter and more than a little jealous, and he didn't even care that he did.

"Quit calling him that." Shayna frowned at him while she sat down at a dressing table nearby and sifted through a jewelry box in search of accessories for her outfit. "And I don't know what you mean by *finally*."

"He's always liked you. I knew that back in high school."

"I don't remember it that way."

Noah didn't mention to her that she hadn't noticed Blake because she was always so focused on him, but then he thought better of it.

Shayna found a pair of small diamond-encrusted hoop earrings. She looked at him in the mirror as she put the earrings on, one by one.

"If I didn't know better, I'd think you were jealous, Noah."

Of course he was jealous, and they both knew it. The question was, *why* was he so jealous. He had been a serial dater while he was overseas—a flavor of the week, as there were so many pretty girls to pick from. Shayna was his friend, not his lover, and he should be happy for his friend if she found someone to date. But he wasn't happy. Not at all.

"Here." He walked over to the dressing table. "Let me help you with that."

Shayna handed him a delicate gold necklace with a single bezel-set diamond. Noah had to force his eyes away from Shayna's alluring cleavage and focus on the tiny necklace clasp. When the necklace was in place, Shayna adjusted the diamond, which nestled nicely between her breasts. If she wanted to draw attention to her assets—and he was sure she did—the diamond was the perfect, twinkling lure for the eyes.

His friend stood up and modeled for him. "Well?"

Wordlessly, mostly because his mouth suddenly went

so dry that his tongue felt like it was stuck to the roof, he gave her a thumb's up.

"You think so?" she asked, taking another look in the full-length mirror.

He nodded. Blake Foreman was a very lucky man. So lucky, in fact, that Noah wanted to punch the guy right in the face.

The doorbell rang, Pilot woofed once and Shayna spun away from him in a cloud of grapefruit and clingy black material. Noah trailed behind Shayna, half wanting to hang back in the shadows and half wanting to insert himself right in the middle of Blake's date with Shayna. After all, Blake might be taking her out, but *he* lived with her. That gave him a home court advantage.

"Hi!" Shayna swung open the door. Her voice filled with sincere excitement.

Blake's eyes looked like they were going to pop right out of his skull at the sight of Shayna in that dress, plunging neckline and all. Noah wanted to throw a blanket over her to stop Blake from sneaking looks at Shayna's ample, alluring bosom.

"Hi, Shayna." Blake smiled at her like she was his favorite dessert. "You look incredible."

Shayna laughed a tinkling feminine laugh that she never used with him; she gave a little twist of her waist. "Body by Blake."

Of course, Blake loved that line, while Noah stewed in the background.

"Shall we?" Blake held out his arm for her to take.

"Absolutely." She hooked her arm with his. "I'm starving."

Blake lifted his chin in a quick acknowledgment that he was standing several paces behind Shayna. "Noah." The trainer said his name in a monotone.

"BB."

Shayna sent him a displeased frown before she turned her sunny smile back to Blake.

"Don't wait up," Shayna threw over her shoulder, and then she was gone.

"Don't worry," Noah muttered as he headed to the kitchen to rummage through the refrigerator. "I *will* wait up."

"I hope you like Italian food."

"Are you kidding me?" She beamed at her tall, hunky escort. "Italian food is one of my love languages."

"Lucky for me." Blake smiled at her as he opened the door for her.

The owner of the Blacksmith Italian Restaurant knew Blake and made sure that they were seated at one of the best tables. At first, Shayna felt a little uneasy about ordering anything other than a salad in front of her trainer, but once Blake ordered risotto fritters and a bottle of sweet red wine, she relaxed into the date and ordered the beef tenderloin and caramelized brussels sprouts.

"I've always wanted to try this place," Shayna said after she had inhaled one of the fritters.

"I'm glad they managed to keep their doors open after the year we've all had."

She nodded, busily chewing another fritter.

"Mmm." She chased the fritter with a sip of red wine. "Such a great way to start."

Blake topped off her wineglass, seeming to enjoy her appreciation of the food. That in itself was a surprise—tonight he wasn't acting like her trainer, he was just acting like a man who found her attractive. She knew he did, because he didn't try to hide it. His attraction to her was written all over his face and in his eyes.

Shayna dabbed her mouth with the napkin and then placed it back in her lap.

"This is a surprise," she said of the date.

Blake looked so handsome in his button-down shirt and fitted slacks. The muscles beneath the cotton of his dress shirt bulged whenever he lifted his glass to take a drink.

He smiled a bit shyly at her, and this shyness in him, with all his handsomeness and gorgeous physique, endeared him to her even more.

"I've been thinking about this for a while."

Even though Noah had told her Blake had had a crush on her for years, she hadn't believed him. But perhaps he had been right—men seemed to spot it in each other long before the woman had a clue.

"You have?" She fiddled with her pendant.

He finished off his wine and took a sip of water with a nod in response.

"So, Dr. Wade." Blake leaned forward, his eyes lingering on her lips for a moment, and when they did, she felt it—butterflies in the stomach. "Tell me about you."

Her hand shook a bit when she picked up her water glass. Lord, Blake Foreman was actually making her heart race. Blake was the first man who wasn't the incomparable Noah Brand who had made her feel nervous and giddy inside. It felt absolutely wonderful.

"What do you want to know?" she said. "You know so much about me already."

She had never noticed before that Blake had a small dimple when he smiled, just like her. Tonight she did, and it registered in her mind that this only added to his considerable appeal.

"Anything," her date countered. "Everything."

The conversation never waned between them, something that Shayna loved about being with Blake. Yes, he was a beefcake now, but growing up he had always been a bookworm who was interested in science and astronomy. Inside that rock-hard chest still beat the heart of a true nerd.

"Thank you so much." Shayna said as Blake came to her chair to hold it out while she stood up. "This was the best meal I've had in a very long time."

"I'll give your compliments to the chef."

"Please do." She smoothed her hand over the skirt of her dress. "That butterscotch budino was literally to die for."

Shayna had topped off her cheat day dinner with a desert that featured Montana caramel sauce, sea salt and homemade vanilla whipped cream that wasn't too sweet.

Together they walked through the restaurant to the

front door, and Shayna noticed that Blake drew the respect of men for the fitness he had achieved and the appreciative eyes of women for exactly the same reason.

Once outside, Blake offered her his arm, and she was happy to link her arm with his.

"Thank you, Blake, I had a wonderful time." Shayna said, wishing the date hadn't sped by so quickly.

Blake caught her eye. "It's not over yet, is it?"

Surprised, her eyes widened. "I don't want it to be over."

"Well, then." Her date put his hand over her fingers resting on his forearm. "That makes two of us."

Chapter Eight

"Hey! Shotgun!" A fit young man out on a date with a college-aged woman waved at Blake. Blake, in turn, lifted up his arms and flexed his biceps as if he were posing during a competition.

"See you at the gym," her date said to the young man.

Once outside, she asked. "Shotgun?"

Blake offered her his arm, and she took it. She felt proud to be escorted by Blake Foreman.

"I guess my nickname got an upgrade since high school," he explained. "The guys on the competition circuit started calling me Shotgun because…"

"You've got two barrels loaded at all times with these arms?" she filled in while simultaneously squeezing his bicep. She had never been so forward with him—so flirtatious—and it felt good.

He put his hand over hers and pulled her just a bit closer. "I always had the biggest arms in the competition. The nickname followed me to my gym."

"Well, I like it."

"A heck of a lot better than BB Gun."

She looked up at his profile. "I never understood that stupid nickname anyway. I told Noah to knock it off."

"You can't blame the guy for getting territorial over you," Blake said. "I would."

"Well," she countered, "I do blame him—he doesn't have any right to be territorial over me. We are, after all, just friends."

They arrived at Blake's loaded GMC truck; he opened the passenger door for her and saw her safely inside. "I'm glad to hear that."

Once he joined her behind the wheel, she prompted him. "So, why BB?"

"My mom loved literature," Blake said, cranking the engine.

"Okay."

"In particular, she loved William Blake and Lord Byron."

"Blake Byron Foreman."

Blake had backed out of the parking spot and shifted into Drive. "At your service."

He pulled out onto the road as he continued. "Once the guys at school found out about my middle name, BB Gun was born. Unfortunately."

"I'm sorry."

He glanced over at her. "It was a long time ago,

Shayna. Name-calling doesn't bother me a bit any-more—when it's aimed at me, that is. They did me a favor, truth be told. I've got thick skin, and I'm hard as a rock on the inside."

"And the outside," she blurted out flirtatiously.

Blake smiled at her compliment, and that smile made her heart begin to race. The man looked good, sounded good with his deep voice, and he smelled really good. He had on subtle cologne that made her senses dance with happiness.

Neither of them was ready to go home, so they headed to the MSU campus to walk off some of their meal.

"Hey, Dr. Wade!" A student waved her down. "Have you uploaded the sign-up sheet for your internship to Google Docs yet?"

Every year, the university allowed her to select a handful of students to get credit for helping her with her Christmas art installation.

"Email me and I'll send you the link," she said.

"What's that all about?" Blake asked her curiously.

"Oh, you know every year I put up an elaborate Christmas display in the front yard of my house. The art department allows me to give up to five students credit for a semester to help me with the installation. The university is allowing them to still intern with me for the fall semester."

"Not a bad gig if you can get it."

She laughed. "Totally."

They found a bench and sat down together. After a

moment, Blake said, "If you need help, I'm really good with my hands." There was a definite sexual undertone in his words, and she blushed when her mind immediately began to wonder what it would feel like to have those big, strong hands touch her all over her body.

"Oh, really?" She said, flirting back. "I might just have to find that out for myself. Maybe do some research."

Noah had been sending her texts periodically during her date; she looked at her phone when it signaled a new text.

"Do you have to go?" Blake asked, probably thinking that she had set up a "get out of this date" signal with a friend.

"Absolutely not." Shayna muted her phone. "It's nothing important."

"How was your date?"

Shayna had come into the house feeling light on her feet and filled with excitement. It had been a wonderful first date—the best first date she had ever had, in fact.

"Oh!" She stopped in her tracks, shoes dangling from the pointer finger of her left hand, the keys to the house in her right hand. "Darn it, Noah! You scared me. What are you doing skulking around in the dark?" She walked over to a nearby lamp. "Turn on some lights, for Pete's sake."

Noah was sitting on the couch in the informal living room, his phone in his hand. He repeated the question, annoyingly. "How was your date?"

"It was *wonderful*."

Noah stood up. "Well, that's wonderful."

Shayna bristled at his tone; she dropped her shoes on the floor and frowned at him. He had managed to suck all the happiness out of the room in less than a minute.

"What's your problem, Noah? Why did you text me eight million times when you knew I was on a date?"

"You don't know?"

"No. Enlighten me," she said, arms crossed defensively in front of her body.

He walked over to her. "You really don't know?"

"I said no, didn't I?"

For the second time that night, a handsome man looked at her lips as if they were succulent morsels that he wanted to sample. When Noah's eyes met hers, they were stormy with emotion, and she, for the first time, couldn't read him like a book.

"Did he kiss you?"

Frustrated, she turned away from him, but he caught her hand and tugged her back onto his realm.

"Did he?"

Frustrated and a little light-headed from the wine, she snapped, "Not that it's any of your business, Noah, but *no*, he didn't kiss me! He's a gentleman, and we both want to take it slow."

Noah growled, "He's an idiot."

She was about to defend Blake's honor when Noah, his hands on the upper part of her arms, pulled her forward, gently but firmly, and kissed her on the lips. There was a split second that her brain thought to push away from Noah, but when he deepened the kiss, holding her so close, her brain went blank and her body went on autopilot. Noah's arms, Noah's lips and Noah's scent enveloped her and time was for a short while suspended while she melted into his arms.

Noah lifted his lips only long enough to say, "Damn it, Shayna. I should have done this years ago."

It took her brain several seconds to override her natural desire to be kissed and held by Noah. Shayna slipped her hands between their bodies and pushed on his chest.

Noah broke the kiss and the embrace. His hands in his pockets, Noah studied her like she was a math problem that he was having difficulty solving.

Feeling numb from head to toe, Shayna stood, very quietly, her arms crossed in front of her body. Neither of them spoke. Shayna spent several seconds trying to make sense of what Noah had just done—he had breached the solid line of friendship that had always been between them.

"Let's talk outside," she said, heading toward the back door of the house.

Noah and Pilot both followed her as she padded her way barefoot across the lawn to the gazebo. Her mind was racing from one thought to another, and nothing seemed to make sense. She had just finished an incredible first date with Blake—a handsome, smart, kind man who was a grown-up and emotionally available. Then she walked in the door and Noah kissed her with all the passion she had only dreamed about for the last twenty years of pining for him.

While Pilot rolled in the sweet-smelling grass, Noah sat down close to her. He tried to take her hand, but she slipped it free from his grasp.

"You're mad at me," he said, but there was a question in his tone.

"No." She gave her typical "don't rock the boat" response, but then she changed her mind. "Actually, yes, I am, Noah."

She looked at his profile. "That was one of the most selfish things I've ever seen you do."

"Selfish?" He appeared genuinely surprised.

"Yes," she reiterated. "Selfish."

"Are we even talking about the same thing, Shay?"

"You kissed me." Shayna said, refusing to give voice to the thoughts *like I always wanted you to*.

Noah turned his body toward her, and the familiar, intoxicating scent of his skin made it difficult for her to maintain her composure. She had always believed that if Noah ever developed romantic feelings for her that she would fling herself at him without thought. It was bizarre to discover that this, in fact, wasn't the case. She wasn't that woman. And if she ever had been, she wasn't anymore.

"I always thought that you wanted me to kiss you, Shay."

Of course, he had known. Everyone in Bozeman knew. She had been making doe eyes at him all her life and tagging along like a dedicated groupie. Perhaps some of the anger she felt was also aimed at herself.

"I did," she said, her tone flat and without emotion. "But not like this."

"Like what?" he asked and attempted to take her hand again.

Shayna stood up, moved to the other side of the gazebo and sat down.

"Like it's a tool."

"A tool? What are you talking about?"

She looked at him directly. "You're jealous. For once, a handsome man is showing an interest in me, and you don't want to lose me."

Noah leaned forward, rubbed his hands over his face several times, and then he leaned his arms on his thighs. "You think that I would actually put our friendship in jeopardy because I don't want you to date Foreman?"

She felt a bit queasy. Noah and she rarely argued, and they had never had such a frank conversation about their relationship. She had worked to keep the peace between them, but tonight she found that she no longer wished to sweep their issues under the rug. If their friendship couldn't survive, then perhaps it had never truly been as solid as she had always believed.

"You're jealous," she reiterated. "You don't want me—" She paused to regain her composure. The memory of years of feeling not good enough for Noah, buried deep within, flooded her body. "But you don't want anyone else to have me, either. That's the truth."

He didn't respond, so she continued quietly, evenly.

"You thought I was about to wiggle off the hook, so you kissed me."

Her words hung in the air between them for several seconds; Noah sat upright, his eyes pinned on her face.

"That's what you think of me?"

She didn't respond. Her chest felt tight, and her throat felt closed off. She was doing something she had avoided for years—she was flirting with the idea of breaking the bond she had always shared with Noah by telling him the unvarnished truth.

"Wow," Noah said angrily. "I must be one hell of a selfish bastard to do something as underhanded as that."

Normally, she would rush to reassure him that he was wonderful and perfect. This time she didn't.

"I kissed you because I wanted to kiss you, Shayna," Noah said. "And I thought, *stupidly*, that you wanted me to kiss you!"

She couldn't deny that—even as recently as a week ago, she would have welcomed his advances. But her date with Blake had impacted her—it had showed her that there was a life out there for her beyond her unrequited love for Noah.

"Now you're giving me the silent treatment?" he asked.

It took several more seconds for her to get the next words out of her mouth. "I think we need some space."

"Meaning?"

"You need to take Isabella to Sugar Creek."

Noah's body went completely still.

"Shayna." He said her name, and she heard genuine undertones of shock and sadness. "You want us to leave?"

She stood up. "Yes."

Shayna hadn't meant to sound so cold, but she couldn't muster any feelings of regret. She had been playing family with Noah and Isabella, and it was time that she forced herself back into reality. If she was going to have a family one day—and she sincerely wanted to have one—she needed to stop fantasizing about Noah and find a man who could return her feelings.

Noah stood up as well and captured the tips of her fingers in his hand.

She paused—didn't pull her fingers away.

"Shayna—all of this over just one kiss?"

"I'm tired." Shayna sighed heavily and tugged her fingers free. "Focus on Isabella, Noah. She's your priority now."

Slowly she walked down the gazebo steps, and she could feel the threads that had always bound them together snapping.

"Shayna. Please." Noah was hurt, but so was she. "I need you."

"No, you don't, Noah," she said, not looking back at him. "You just think you do."

"She's stopped talking to me." Noah was sitting in his mother's sewing room. Isabella was loving her "vacation" at Sugar Creek and had already blended in with the family. Today, she was at Bruce and Savannah's house, which had given him some time alone with his mother.

Lilly's hands continued to work the suede that she used to create moccasins, which she sold on the reservation and on her website.

"Why has she stopped talking to you?" his mother asked.

All of Noah's most important talks with his mother had happened in her garden or in her sewing room. When he was in his mother's world, he found it almost impossible to lie.

"I kissed her."

Lilly's wise dark eyes lifted from her work. "I see."

"Do you?" he asked, frustrated. "Because I sure don't. She's always wanted more from me than just friendship. And then when I give it to her, she cuts me off!"

Lilly's lips turned up in to a small smile. "Shayna is a very smart woman."

Noah waited for her mother to continue.

"If she's not talking to you, you gave her ample reason."

He stood up and walked over to the window overlooking a herd of cattle grazing as far as the eye could see. "Why is everyone speaking in riddles?"

Lilly put down her work. "Why did you kiss her, Noah? Why now, after all of these years?"

Several answers rose to the front of his mind, but none seemed like legitimate reasons for him to have crossed that line of friendship with Shayna. When he couldn't seem to pinpoint one specific, compelling reason, and as he remained silent in thought, Lilly returned to her work.

"This is why she is not talking to you, son," his mother said simply. "You are not children anymore. If you want her back in your life…"

"I do." He missed her terribly. Even when he had been overseas, he only needed to pick up the phone to hear her voice. Shayna had always been on the other end of the line.

"Then you must decide what you want," Lilly said. "It seems that Shayna has lost patience with being put on the shelf like a forgotten toy. And I, for one, support her one hundred percent."

Shayna had spent her week without Noah focusing on her Christmas display. Immersing herself into the holiday spirit always lifted her mood. Yes, she missed him. Of course, she did. But, surprisingly, she hadn't shed a tear.

"What do you think about this, Dr. Wade?" Steve, one of her undergraduate interns, showed her a mock-up of one of her life-size princesses.

Shayna scanned the dimensions on the sketch, which included a materials list. "It's perfect. Can you get started once I have ordered the materials?"

The intern nodded. "Absolutely. I'm excited about it."

Once she approved of the final mock-ups of all the princesses, Shayna said goodbye to the interns and got herself ready to leave for the local home improvement store. The managers and sales personnel would know, the minute they saw her walk in, that it was time to start ordering all the supplies for her Christmas display.

"You be a good boy." Shayna knelt down beside Pilot's bed and dropped a kiss between his ears.

Shayna decided to drive the Chevelle. Driving her dream car was similar to involving herself in anything Christmas—it lifted her spirits. She drove with the windows rolled down, loving the feeling of the warm late-summer air on her skin. Wisps of hair that had escaped from her high ponytail swirled around her face while she sang along to one of her favorite Fleetwood Mac songs. She was singing loudly and off-key when her phone rang.

"Hey, Blake!" she yelled at him over the music. "Hold on!"

She could hear him laughing, a sound that she had grown to like very much, while she fumbled to turn down the volume.

"Sorry about that," she said, finally managing to lower the volume to a whisper. "I love me some Fleetwood Mac."

"Stevie Nicks," Blake agreed.

"Totally."

They laughed again. It wasn't lost on her that Noah had been making her feel sad and frustrated and unappreciated lately, while Blake made her feel interesting, and desirable, and *fun*.

"I'm sorry that I had to cancel this week," the trainer said.

"That's okay."

Blake surprised her when he said, "I missed you."

Shayna hesitated but then said, "You know what, I missed you, too. I was just thinking about that today."

Oddly, she had had a week without Noah and Blake, and she had missed them both—each for different reasons, but she had missed them equally.

"I'm glad to hear that," Blake said without trying to hide his true feelings. She really appreciated that about him.

Shayna blushed with pleasure at his words. She was glad to hear that he had missed her as well.

Blake filled in the silence with a question. "What have you been up to?"

She smiled. "I've actually been working on getting things rolling on my display."

"Oh, yeah? How's that going?"

Excitedly, she said, "All of my interns have been by the house to get a feel for the site. The mock-ups are done, and now I'm on my way to order supplies."

Blake asked her more questions about the display, and she felt happy to share the details with him. He sounded genuinely interested in her project.

"It sounds like you're off to a great start," he said. "I can't believe I've missed this display of yours for all of these years."

"I can't, either!" she exclaimed. "It's a really big deal."

Blake laughed with her, and then he said, "I hope this doesn't mean that you're going to put training on the back burner."

"No." Shayna pulled into the parking lot. "I'll still see you next week as usual."

"Good," he said. "But actually, a week seems like a really long time from now. I was hoping to see you before that."

She shifted into Park and shut off the engine. Her heart began to pound in anticipation. This sounded like Blake was about to ask her for a second date, and she *wanted* him to ask.

"Oh, yeah?"

"Yeah," he said. "Would you like to go out to the movies with me Friday night?"

"A Friday-night date?" she teased. "That's pretty serious, you know. Next level."

"Ready or not?"

With a huge smile on her face, Shayna said, "I'm ready."

Chapter Nine

"You should call her again." Isabella was walking with a long stride, stomping her feet loudly each time they landed on the pavement.

His mom had braided Isabella's hair into two long plaits, and his daughter was wearing tan boots, jeans and a sequined unicorn T-shirt. He loved Isabella without thought, but he was always grateful when his family occupied her time. It was going to take a lot of adjustment to become a full-fledged father. He just wasn't used to having a little person tagging along after him.

"I did call her," Noah said as they walked through the sliding doors of the store.

"Call her again," his daughter said, stomping her feet.

"Could you please stop stomping your feet?" Noah asked. "It's rude."

Isabella frowned at him, and when she did, it was Annika's face that stared back at him.

"I need to help with the princesses. Shayna said so."

His daughter was pouting, and honestly, he might have pouted, too, if he wasn't an adult and a marine to boot. Shayna's determination not to forgive him was unprecedented. He'd been able to charm, wink and cajole his way out of trouble with Shayna since they were kids. In his mind, he blamed Blake for his current trouble with Shayna, but in his heart, he knew that it was all on his shoulders.

"Look, I know you want to help with the princesses. Shayna's been busy. That's all."

Isabella swung her arms wildly, clopping along beside him in her boots.

"We should go to her house," Isabella said. "Maybe she lost her phone."

Noah had to admit that he had considered stopping by Shayna's house—but he also had to admit that this new version of Shayna kind of scared him. He was already in hot water with her—if he was going to find a way forward with Shayna, he was going to have to be more strategic. And it was that thought that had turned into a plan. Shayna had a soft spot for Christmas, and her Christmas village was probably the most prized of all her possessions, even more than her vintage muscle car. He had already promised to build her a wraparound shelf for her village; if he showed up at her house bearing supplies for the shelf *and* with Isabella in tow, perhaps he had a better than fifty percent chance of not having the door slammed in his face.

"Let's head over to the lumber department," he told Isabella, whose eyes had just grown very large at the sight of a display of gourmet lollipops.

"Can I have a lollipop?" Isabella's head swiveled around even though her legs were still moving forward.

"No."

"Why not?"

"Because I said so." Noah actually frowned at the words that just flew out his mouth without thought. "Wow. It took me less than a month to become my father," he muttered.

"Call Nanna and ask her," Isabella bargained.

"You know what?"

"What?"

"If you stop stomping your feet for the rest of the time we are in this store, I'll buy you two lollipops."

Isabella looked up at him with her impish little face and intelligent blue eyes. "Really?"

"Really."

Yes, he had bribed her, but now she wasn't stomping her feet. So, for him, it was a checkmark in the win column.

He was still feeling pretty satisfied with his own ability to parent when Isabella shouted, "Shayna!" and took off up the aisle.

Noah faltered a step when he saw Shayna standing in front of the large sheets of plywood.

"Shayna!" Isabella called out again as she barreled

toward Shayna and, when she reached her, flung herself into her arms.

Surprised, Shayna closed her arms around Isabella and gave her a bear hug.

Noah took in the sight of his best friend and his daughter. Shayna's face had a glow of happiness; her long, wispy hair was mussed and tendrils were slipping free from her haphazard ponytail. She was wearing faded jeans with holes at the knees and splattered paint stains. The jeans hugged her curvy hips, and the Montana State University T-shirt equally emphasized her assets. Shayna was beautiful; Shayna was sexy. And his body was responding to her as a woman, not as a friend. In that moment, Noah had complete clarity.

"Hi, Shayna." He stopped a few feet away.

"Hi." She smiled at him, and that smile reached her pretty green eyes.

"I found her." Isabella was holding on to Shayna's hand. It seemed to him that perhaps both of them, his daughter and himself, had missed Shayna more than they had realized.

"I see this."

"How are you?" his best friend asked him.

Very aware that Isabella's ears were tuned into their conversation, Noah said only, "Glad to see you."

"Are you working on the princesses?" Isabella asked, still holding Shayna's hand.

Shayna bent her head down and gave his daughter a sweet, kind smile that touched him unexpectedly.

"Yes, I have been."

Isabella frowned and looked as if she were about to start crying. "But I was supposed to help you."

Shayna's face crumpled, and she hugged Isabella tightly again. "There's still plenty to do, I promise. Today I'm getting the wood, but I still have to test all of my lights. And you—" Shayna tapped Isabella's shoulder gently "—need to help me decide which new lights I need to order."

It amazed him how easily Shayna was able to change Isabella's mood. He had never thought about it, but Shayna had a natural gift with children. She certainly had a special way with his daughter.

"Did Lilly put you to work?" Shayna asked him.

"No." He smiled at her, feeling so happy, relieved and excited to be talking to Shayna again.

"We're getting stuff for your Christmas village," Isabella piped up, letting go of Shayna and skipping around in a little circle.

"Is that right?"

Noah felt a bit sheepish when he said, "I thought it might…"

"Get me to open my door?" she asked in a whisper, out of earshot of Isabella.

"Would it work?" he asked with a grin.

Shayna gave one cute little shrug of her shoulder. "Maybe."

The meeting at the local home improvement store had served as the icebreaker Noah needed to get his foot back in Shayna's door. For the next two days, he worked on Shayna's Christmas village display shelf while Isabella and Shayna tested yards and yards of strings of lights. They hadn't broached the subject of *the kiss*, but every time he looked at her, he was reminded of how soft and sweet her lips had felt. With just that one kiss, Noah had felt the earth shift beneath his feet for a second time: first when he met Isabella, and the second time when he had kissed Shayna as a man would kiss a woman he desired.

"What is this?" Noah walked into Shayna's art studio. "Are the two of you playing while I do all the work?"

"I'm painting," Isabella said proudly as she tried to copy the strokes Shayna was making on her own canvas.

"I see this," Noah said, amused by the fact that now his daughter had paint on her fingers and her clothing, and there was even a spot on her nose that matched the spot of purple on Shayna's nose.

Shayna turned her head and smiled at him. "We're taking a little break."

Shayna had set Isabella up with her own easel, canvas, paintbrushes and paints right next to her own workstation. Pilot had joined them, with his large body sprawled out next to Isabella. Noah watched them interact for a minute, and it never failed—whenever he saw Shayna being kind to his daughter and going out of her way to make Isabella feel special, Noah felt like his best friend was the most wonderful woman in the world. He had met so many beautiful women in his world travels, but none could compare with the beauty he saw in Shayna's heart.

Noah walked around the room where Shayna spent hours of her day creating paintings of the Montana landscape. His friend had always been fascinated by Montana foliage and the wildlife. Shayna's recent collection focused on the wildflowers that brought so much color and life to the fields and streams and mountains of her beloved Montana.

"What are you hiding under here?" Noah stopped by a canvas that was covered by a large piece of muslin.

"I'm trying a new technique," Shayna said simply with a little shrug. "I'm just not ready to show it yet."

Isabella made a frustrated noise and frowned when her brushstroke didn't match Shayna's. "I can't do it right."

"Yes, you can, sweet pea." Shayna used a calm, reassuring tone of voice. "It just takes practice."

"I think you're doing great, Isabella." Noah stopped just behind their stools.

"Don't give up," his friend added and then asked, "How are things going on your end?"

"You mean, how are things going for the person in this house who's actually been working?" he teased her. "I'm pretty proud of it. When you get a chance, come look for yourself."

Shayna nodded. Before she followed him into the formal living room at the front of the house, she put her hand over Isabella's and guided her hand to make strokes on the canvas. After several strokes, Shayna removed her hand and let Isabella try on her own. For her efforts, Shayna was rewarded with a huge smile and a tinkling laugh from his daughter.

"I did it!" Isabella exclaimed.

"Yes, you did," Shayna agreed as she stood up. "This should show you that you should never give up."

"Thank you for doing that for her," Noah said once they were out of Isabella's earshot.

"I was doing it as much for me as I was for her."

"I doubt that."

He looked over at her profile, noticing all the little details of her face: her straight nose, the set of her chin, the small gold paintbrush earrings that she liked to wear. The skin on her cheeks and the bridge of her nose was sunburned because she had spent time in her yard weeding by hand without a hat on. Tendrils of honey-mahogany hair curled down her long neck in the most attractive way; her standard haphazard bun was slowly falling apart, and Noah was tempted to reach up and let her hair loose. He wanted to bury his hands in her hair and his nose in her neck. But now that the tables had turned and Shayna had put him solidly in the friend zone while she explored her new feelings for Blake, Noah couldn't help but fear that he had missed a once-in-a-lifetime opportunity with her.

"Wow!" Shayna stopped in her tracks when she saw the work he had done on her wrap-around-the-room shelf for her Christmas village.

Noah loved the genuine surprise and happiness he

saw on her face. He felt like he could spend a lifetime finding ways to make her pretty face glow as it was now.

Shayna had tears of joy in her eyes.

"Thank you." She threw her arms around him and hugged him tightly.

This was the first time since the kiss that the invisible barrier between them had been broken. Noah took advantage of the moment and wrapped his arms around her and rested his chin on the top of her head as he had always liked to do.

"I'm glad you like it, Shay."

Shayna gave him one last squeeze before she went to take a closer look at the shelf that now wrapped around the entire formal living room.

"It's exactly what I wanted," she said. "You're so talented, Noah."

He walked up beside her. "So you approve?"

"It's better than I imagined. I love it."

Shayna looked up into his face with so much love and appreciation that all Noah could think about was kissing her again. For a split second, there was an electric charge between them; their eyes were locked, his body felt like it was being pulled toward hers, and when Shayna licked her lips, it was almost his undoing. He wanted to kiss her again; he had never wanted to kiss anyone as much as he wanted to kiss Shayna. And in his gut, he believed that if he kissed her, Shayna would not push him away this time.

Noah moved his head in her direction, and she didn't pull away. The doorbell ringing broke the spell.

"Oh, no! What time is it?" Shayna looked over at the grandfather clock in the corner.

Noah cursed silently but was careful not to let the frustration show on his face.

His friend left him in the living room and walked quickly to the door. When she opened it, he heard Blake's voice, and when he did, Noah balled up his fists and couldn't believe his rotten luck. Of course, just when he was beginning to make some progress with Shayna.

"BB Gun shows up," Noah muttered under his breath.

"Oh my goodness, Blake!" Shayna felt hot and flushed when she opened her front door. "I completely lost track of time!"

Blake took off his sunglasses so she could see his eyes. He smiled at her warmly. "I'm glad to see you."

Shayna's heart did a little skip. There was something about Blake that made her feel like a giddy school-girl. But the glow she felt on her face was a direct result of the moment she had just shared with Noah. She knew that Noah wanted to kiss her—he had *intended* to kiss her—and there was a very large part of her body and brain that *wanted* those kisses from Noah. Perhaps Blake interrupting that almost kiss was the universe sending her a sign to stand her ground and keep Noah safely in the friend zone.

"I'm glad to see you too," she said with a nervous laugh. "Come on in. I just need to change real quick."

Blake stepped inside her world, and he seemed to

make everything appear just a little bit smaller and more cramped.

"It looks like a Christmas store exploded in here," the trainer mused.

"I know!" She clasped her hands together excitedly. "Isn't it wonderful?"

Noah was still in the formal living room, packing up his tools.

"Noah has been building a display shelf for my Christmas village." She sounded nervous, and she wished she didn't.

Why did she feel like she had done something wrong by having Noah over? It wasn't like she had an exclusive relationship with Blake. They had only been on two dates, and he hadn't even tried to kiss her yet. The furthest they had gone was holding each other's hands. And Shayna was happy to take it slowly—especially when she had so many mixed emotions about her relationship with Noah. Until she made peace with her feelings for Noah, Shayna was certain she couldn't be a good partner to any man.

"Don't forget, I'm pretty handy with my tools," Blake reminded her.

"I haven't forgotten," she said quickly. "I'm definitely going to need all the extra hands I can get when we start to install the display."

"Foreman." Noah jerked his chin in Blake's direction.

"Brand." The trainer didn't sound too pleased to find Noah in her house.

"I'll be right back," she said, wanting to change into

her workout clothes as quickly as she could possibly manage and get back to Blake. She didn't like the idea of Noah spending too much time alone with the man she had recently begun to date. It just seemed too *messy*.

"Where are you going?" Isabella came out of her art studio and trailed behind her.

"I'm going to exercise with Blake."

"Can I come?"

"No, love. I think your—" she almost let the word *dad* slip out "—Noah is getting ready to take you back to Sugar Creek."

"Okay." The young girl sounded disappointed.

Shayna paused from her mission and gave the girl a long hug. "I'll see you soon. We have more work to do, and I need your help."

Isabella seemed pleased. "And I can do more painting."

"Of course." Shayna gave her one last hug. "Take Pilot outside for me, okay?"

Noah's daughter nodded her head and then skipped down the hallway toward the art studio, where Pilot was still lounging.

Shayna quickly changed into her workout clothes, ran a brush through her hair and pulled it up into a high ponytail, and then tried to scrub the paint off her face. She raced out of her room and made a beeline for the formal living room.

"Shayna."

When she heard her name, she switched direction and headed to her studio.

"These are incredible." Blake was admiring her work.

"Thank you," she said. "I'm trying to get ready for a show."

"You're incredible, Shayna," Blake said.

"I think you're incredible," she replied without much thought.

Isabella, romping in the backyard, executing impressive handstands while Pilot lolled nearby in the cool grass, caught Blake's attention.

"Is that…" Blake stared hard at Isabella. "Annika's daughter?"

"Yes." She tried to sound nonchalant. "That's Isabella."

Blake gave her a curious look.

"It's a long story," she said, and she knew that her little laugh sounded nervous.

Blake looked at Isabella again. "I think I've already read the CliffsNotes."

Blake had been the valedictorian of their high school—and just because he was a beefcake now didn't mean he wasn't one of the most intelligent men she had ever known. Of course, he could put two and two together. Gratefully, Blake didn't care much for town gossip and dropped the topic.

"You'll lock up for me?" Shayna asked Noah on her way out.

"Yep."

Shayna couldn't help but notice that Noah seemed a bit forlorn, and her natural instinct was to find a way to make him feel better. She had to deliberately remind herself of the years she had watched Noah walk out the door with Annika.

"Thank you, Noah. I love the shelf."

He looked up from his chore; the look in his eyes could only be described as worried and upset. "Anything for you."

For a second or two, she was caught up in Noah's gaze and everything—everyone—disappeared. The sound of Blake's keys jingling in his pocket snapped her back to the present.

"Where are you taking me today?" she asked, hoping that her cheeks weren't as red as the nose on Rudolph the reindeer.

"I thought we'd go to the park. I have some new exercises to show you."

Shayna walked through the door that Blake held open for her.

"Oh, goody!" She said teasingly, "I was hoping for new exercises today."

And just when she had thought Blake hadn't noticed the electricity between Noah and her minutes before, Blake captured her hand as they walked to his truck and said, "Anything for you."

Shayna had fallen asleep with the lights on and her reading glasses still on the top of her head. After her workout with Blake, they had gone out for a light dinner, and then she had returned home to dive back into research for the book she was going to write. Somewhere along the way, Pilot had joined her in the bed and she had ended up hugging the dog like an over-size stuffed animal. When her phone rang, it took her a minute to place herself properly in space and time. It was dark outside, so it was nighttime or very early in the morning.

She groggily turned over, struggling a bit because Pilot was sleeping on a part of her T-shirt.

"Darn it, Pilot!" She tried to tug free of the dog's weight. Pilot kept on snoring, completely oblivious of the fact that she was basically trapped.

She finally freed herself, rolled over awkwardly and then searched under the stacks of papers on her nightstand to find her phone. Right when she found the phone, it stopped ringing.

"Darn it! Where are my glasses?" Shayna looked under the papers on the bed and on the nightstand. And then she felt on top of her head and there they were.

She looked at her phone and saw that Noah had been the one to call her, and it was nearly midnight.

She propped up on her pillows and dialed his number. Pilot continued to snore loudly next to her.

"Shayna." Noah answered the phone with a tense voice.

"Noah. What's wrong?"

"I just got a call from the rehab facility. May was transported to the hospital."

Shayna had to process that information for a second or two before she asked the obvious question. "Why?"

"I don't have all of the details yet. I took Isabella to see her today after we left your house. She wasn't feeling well. She was complaining about feeling off, but she thought it was because of how hard she had been working in physical therapy."

"Why did they call you?"

"I'm listed as her next of kin."

"I didn't realize."

"Neither did I."

Shayna supposed it made sense for May to list Noah as her contact. After all, Annika, as far as they knew, was still at a drug and alcohol rehab facility. If they did contact her, what could she do?

Noah sighed heavily on the other end of the line. He sounded so weary.

"What are you going to do, Noah?"

"I don't know," he said pensively. "There's too much to do and not enough time to do it. I'm working with the lawyer to establish paternity. I haven't even begun to deal with Annika—not that I want to deal with her in the first place."

Shayna could hear the sincerity in his voice—Noah did not want to have anything to do with his ex-fiancée. But, sooner or later, deal with her he must. She was, after all, the mother of his child.

"I was hoping that maybe May would be out of rehab before I have to leave, and with the right amount of help, she would be able to take care of Isabella until I could get myself sorted out."

"Your leave is almost over," she said as much to herself as to him.

"I know." Noah sighed again. "After tonight, I think

I'm going to have to ask for an extension of my hardship leave. Things are just too complicated. I can't leave until all of the pieces are on the board."

"What can I do to help, Noah?"

"Will you go with me to see May in the hospital tomorrow?"

Both of them, Shayna believed, were aware that the kiss *had* changed things between them. But they were both also completely willing to ignore that big, fat elephant in the room, sweep the issue right under the carpet and pretend like things were exactly the same as they always had been *prekiss.*

"Of course, I will." For better or for worse, Noah Brand was still—at least for now—her best and oldest friend.

Chapter Ten

"Thank you for coming with me today," Noah said.

They were sitting in her driveway after visiting May in the hospital.

"I was glad you asked me."

Several seconds of silence unfolded, and Shayna had to believe that they were thinking the same thing.

"She didn't look good." Noah put a voice to her thoughts.

"No."

"I don't think I should tell Isabella."

It was a statement, but Shayna heard a question in his words.

"I wouldn't," she said. "Isabella doesn't need to be worried about her grandmother right now. May could go back to the rehab facility tomorrow, for all we know."

"She is a tough old bird." Noah attempted to lighten the mood.

"That she is."

When they both fell silent again, Shayna gathered up her purse and her phone. "Well, I guess I'd better head inside. A geriatric Great Dane with a full bladder is never a good idea."

Noah reached out and touched her arm. "Hold on a sec."

Shayna still had her hand on the door handle while she waited for Noah to continue.

Noah turned his body toward her; he was still the most handsome man she had ever seen, but he had dark circles under his eyes now and he seemed to have aged several years over the last couple of weeks.

"I'd like us to go to dinner."

Shayna looked at Noah with an expression, she was sure, that read *why are you being a weirdo?*

They had been out to eat umpteen thousands of times. They'd been to breakfast, brunch, lunch and dinner and shared drunken midnight snacks.

"You've never been so oddly formal about it, but sure. I'll grab a bite with you and Isabella. When were you thinking?"

Noah stared at her, and she stared back at him.

"I think we are having a failure to communicate," he said.

"We probably are, because you are acting like a crazy person."

"Let me try this again."

She waited.

"I'm asking you out on a date, Shayna," Noah said seriously. "Will you go out to dinner with me?"

Now she was frowning at him. Wordlessly, she opened the door to the truck, got out and slammed the door shut. She heard Noah's door open and shut; she heard his cowboy boots on the concrete as he chased after her.

At her front door, Shayna fumbled with the keys until she finally got the correct key into the keyhole. She hated the fact that her hands were shaking. She opened the door, stepped inside and then faced Noah.

"Go home, Noah. I'm not getting into this with you right now."

"Getting into what?" he demanded of her. "What do you think I'm trying to do here?"

Shayna threw up her hands. "That would be getting into it, now wouldn't it?"

Noah thought about turning and leaving, but he just couldn't. Everything in his life was taking on a new urgency and new seriousness, and he needed to deal with his feelings for Shayna one way or another. Instead of heading back to a Sugar Creek Ranch truck he'd been driving, Noah followed her into the house, shut the door behind him and then fell into formation behind Pilot, who was moving stiffly and very, very slowly toward the backyard.

Shayna had thrown her purse unceremoniously on the kitchen counter, and she had kicked her shoes off before she headed out the back door. She was ticked off at him, but he was willing to face the music as long as he could face it with Shayna. At night, when he couldn't sleep for worrying about Isabella and having to go back overseas, and dreading having Annika back in his life, his mind would inevitably turn to Shayna. Sweet, loving, steady-as-a-rock Shayna—he had always taken her for granted. He had always just assumed that she would be there for him unconditionally. Blake Foreman had shown him how wrong he was. His friendship with Shayna was as fragile as the glass Christmas ornaments she loved so much. It could be shattered if he didn't handle it with care.

Shayna headed straight to the gazebo, and he followed. He sat down across from her, wanting to give her some space even as he wanted to push her into addressing the unspoken tension between them.

"You're mad at me."

"Very observant." Her sarcasm wasn't lost on him, and normally he would feed into it, but right now, he had to keep a cool head. He couldn't risk pushing her farther away from him.

"Talk to me, Shayna," Noah said gently. "Why are you so mad? I want to take you out. Why is that such a bad thing? As far as I know, you aren't exclusive with Foreman."

Shayna narrowed her eyes at him. "I'm not going to talk to you about Blake, Noah."

He crossed his arms in front of his body and then forced himself to uncross his arms and remain open to

Shayna in his mind and with his body language. "Okay. Then let's talk about us."

"Us?" She scoffed. "What *us* are you talking about Noah? You know, I was willing, mostly for Isabella's sake, to move past the line you crossed the other night. But now I'm really beginning to wonder if that was such a hot idea. If I give you an inch, you take a mile. Same old Noah."

Noah scooted forward on the bench and leaned in to the conversation. "No. Not same old Noah. Shayna, can't you see? I'm different. Isabella has changed me... for the better. I just wish you could see it."

Shayna frowned at him; her eyes were shuttered, and he couldn't seem to read her as well as he had been before. His friend had become somewhat of a mystery to him—a challenging puzzle he couldn't seem to solve. And then something struck him like a lightning bolt to the brain. If he wanted to move the needle at all with Shayna, he was going to have to put all his cards on the table. No holding back.

"I love you, Shayna." Noah said.

"I know you do, Noah," she said, her face unsmiling, her eyes wary. "I love you, too."

"No." He reached out across the small divide between them and took her hands into his hands. "I'm *in love* with you, Shayna."

Shayna's body went completely still, and Noah saw her inhale quickly and hold her breath. Their eyes locked, and Noah didn't try to hide what his soul was feeling for her. In fact, he wanted for her to see his love for her. No more hiding—at least not from Shayna.

For a split second, Noah saw tears begin to form in her eyes, but, in usual Shayna fashion, she pushed down the emotions that were behind the tears and stopped even one drop from falling onto her cheeks.

Without ceremony, she tugged her fingers free and put her hands in her lap.

Noah watched her closely; it appeared to him that she was trying to find the right words. And if it was taking her this long, he highly doubted that Shayna was going to say *I'm in love with you, too.*

Shayna's head was bowed, and then she breathed in deeply, let it out slowly and then met his gaze.

"You've been through a life-changing event, Noah. Annika and Isabella have turned your life upside down and sideways. You became a father overnight, and now you're wondering how you're going to balance your duty as a marine and your duty as a father."

Noah leaned back, sensing that this was not going in his direction.

"You're confused, Noah. I can't blame you for that. I don't think anyone could blame you." She pointed to her chest. "But you aren't in love with me."

He had to stop himself from interrupting and protesting. He *wasn't* confused.

"I've always been a safe place for you to land. Ever since we were kids. Of course you would want to find safe harbor with me, and I think that my relationship with Blake is a threat to that safe place. But I can't be your consolation prize, Noah. It's not healthy for me."

Noah wasn't often shocked into silence, but Shayna could always make him feel things that no one else could. Her stark assessment of his declaration of love hurt. And yet, he had to acknowledge that he had been the one to take her for granted. Noah rubbed his hand over his face several times before he spoke.

"You doubt that I'm in love with you." It was a statement and a question all wrapped up in one.

"I doubt it because it's not true. You've been here for three weeks, Noah. You've been under an enormous amount of pressure. My best advice is to find a good therapist for Isabella and you."

"You're right, Shay. My world has been blown up thanks to Annika. But that doesn't mean I've lost my ability to think and feel. I have always loved you as a friend. Always. And now, whether you like it or not, I'm in love with you."

"Stop saying that."

"No." His brow furrowed at her sheer stubbornness. "I won't stop saying it, Shayna, because it's the truth. I fell in love with you, and I have to tell you, it came as quite a surprise to me as well."

She didn't respond, and he could read the expression on her face: she remained unconvinced.

"Do you love him? Is that why you're putting up every barrier between us that you can think of?"

"I'm not going to discuss Blake with you. I believe we've already covered that."

"Do. You. Love. Him?" he repeated, overemphasizing each word. "After all we have been through together, don't we at least owe each other honesty?"

"I've always been honest with you."

"Yes. You have."

Shayna locked eyes with him. "No. I'm not in love with him. Not yet. But I know that I could be."

That familiar knot of worry twisted in his gut. He didn't want to admit how appealing Blake was to Shayna. Unfortunately, the guy, who had far from peaked in high school, was nothing like the scrawny science nerd they all once knew.

"Then why not give us a shot, Shayna?" he asked. "What do you have to lose?"

"What do I have to lose?" She repeated the question with a razor-sharp edge in her voice. "How about *everything*? My heart, my dreams, my sex life! What am I supposed to do when you go back overseas? Tie a yellow ribbon around a tree in my front yard and hold a candlelight vigil every night waiting for you to return? Why in the world would I do that to myself? Seriously, Noah? Do you even know what you're asking? You're asking me to start up a long-distance relationship with a man—"

"Your best friend," he inserted.

"—who I am sure has no intention of staying celibate for months at a time. I would have to be absolutely nuts, and I can assure you, I'm *not*."

"Now I think—"

"I'm not finished." Shayna scooted forward and

pinned him with an expression he'd never seen on her face before. She wasn't trying to smooth anything over this time; she wasn't trying to spare his feelings. "And meanwhile, you've got a storm with Annika brewing on the horizon.

"So let me see—why would I exchange my peaceful, organized, normal life for all the crazy you've got going on?" She tilted her head to the side caustically. "I think I'll pass."

"So that's it?" he asked, his anger and frustration bubbling to the surface. "You just dismiss me like I'm a nobody. Like I'm just some guy off the street?"

Shayna stood up. "Honestly, Noah, if you don't like it, it's just too damn bad."

Noah stood up as well. "Where is the Shayna that I know?"

"She's right here."

"Where is she?"

Shayna's voice ticked up a notch. "I'm *right* here!"

It took a significant amount of control not to grab her and kiss her. He knew that she loved him. He *knew* it—in his heart and in his gut and in his mind. She loved him as much as he loved her. She was just too blasted scared to admit it.

"You love me, Shayna." Noah lowered his volume deliberately to a more intimate level. "You're in love with me."

She shook her head in denial, breaking their eye contact and turning her head away from him.

He gently lifted her chin so he could look directly

into her eyes. "I wish I hadn't been so blind, Shayna. All of this time, I never saw the woman who was meant to be my forever. I don't know why it took me so long. I don't know why it took finding out about Isabella for everything to come into focus. But that's what happened, Shayna. Please believe me."

The unshed tears were back in his beloved's eyes, and he knew that he was the cause of her pain.

"Please forgive me, Shayna."

She cleared her throat. "There isn't anything to forgive you for, Noah."

"Yes." He tucked a wayward lock of hair behind her ear. "Yes, there is."

"I forgive you."

He took her hands in his and kissed the back of each one and then held on to them. "Tell me that you still love me, Shayna. Tell me that it isn't too late for us."

One tear did escape from her eyes, and he was quick to wipe it away.

"I hate that I've made you cry, Shayna. I hate it." Noah heard the sincerity in his own voice and only hoped that Shayna, who knew him better than anyone, would hear it as well. "You're in love with me, Shayna. You are. I know you are, because I feel it in my heart. With every beat, I feel your love for me." He put her hand over his heart. "Right here."

"Why are you doing this to me, Noah?" There was so much heartbreak in her voice that it almost brought him to his knees. He had been so wrong for so many years. How could he possibly make it up to her? He didn't know, but he had to try.

"Tell me that you're in love with me, Shayna." Noah pleaded with her; he had never pleaded with anyone before. "Put me out of my misery."

"I'm in love with you," she whispered. "I always have been."

He held her face in his hands, wanting to memorize every angle of her face and hold it in his mind and heart for the rest of his days.

"I always will be," Shayna said and there was poignancy in her tone that made him want to prove every doubt she had about him wrong.

"Then kiss me, Shayna," Noah said. "Kiss the man who loves you as much as you love him."

His love tilted her head back, and he lowered his so that their lips touched. It was a tender, sweet kiss— a promise from him to her. He wrapped her up in his arms, breathed in the fresh scent of her hair and reveled in the softness of her skin. Noah dropped butterfly kisses on her cheeks, on her forehead, and then he returned to her lips. The taste of her, the feel of her in his arms was more intoxicating than any liquor he'd ever tried. Shayna was finally in his arms. He didn't deserve her. Not yet. But he fully intended to spend the rest of his life proving himself worthy of this woman.

Shayna held on to him tightly, her head resting on his rapidly beating heart.

"This is a dream," she said so quietly that he almost didn't hear the words.

Noah closed his eyes and rested his chin on the top of her head. "Then don't wake up, Shay. Just keep on dreaming."

Shayna hadn't felt so nervous in years. The last time she could remember feeling sick with nerves was when she had to defend her dissertation in order to earn her PhD. Now, she was getting ready for her first official date with Noah, something she had dreamed about since she was a preteen, and her body was buzzing with anxiety. She had allowed herself the luxury of taking a long, hot bubble bath. There was something about soaking in a tub and the slipperiness of her naked skin when she was in the bath that made her feel sexy. And she wanted to feel sexy when she went out on this date with Noah. The hot bath served to calm her nerves, but she still felt jittery when she stepped out of the bathtub to dry herself off. Once dry, she stood in front of the full-length mirror in the bathroom and dropped the towel. Shayna examined herself closely, turning from side to side and then looking at her body straight on. She ran her hands over her breasts, down the curve of her waist, across her stomach and down her thighs. For the first time in her life, she felt good in her own skin.

No, she would never be super thin, and she didn't want to be—she was a solid size ten now, and it felt perfect to her. She had large breasts, wider hips and thick thighs. But her waist was defined, her muscles toned and she felt that her hourglass figure was voluptuous. Her stomach, the last problem area that still needed some work, didn't detract from the shapeliness of her figure. If she ever were naked in front of Noah, she would be proud. She would be happy to leave the lights on and give Noah a show he wouldn't soon forget.

"Body by Blake." She gave herself one last look in the mirror before she donned a robe.

For the entire day leading up to her date with Noah, Blake had been on her mind. No, they weren't exclusive and they were still, basically, in the platonic stage of their relationship; yet, she felt guilty. If this experiment with Noah didn't crash and burn epically, she would have to do the hard thing and let Blake know that her friendship with Noah had evolved into a romance.

"A romance with Noah Brand," Shayna said in a lilting voice as she searched her closet for the perfect first-date outfit. She had a couple of dresses in mind, but she hadn't settled on *the one*.

Finally, she decided to wear a forest green dress that hugged her curves and emphasized her cleavage. The dress fell just above the knee; the skirt flared and swung when she walked, drawing attention to her rounded derriere. She chose a strappy pair of heels that showed off her shapely calves. She had just finished applying her makeup when the doorbell rang.

"He's early!" she exclaimed. She still needed to finish her hair. She quickly removed the tissue paper that she had placed in her armpits to stop her sweating from nerves and excitement to stain her dress before she walked quickly to the front door. She had no intention of opening the door for him, but she didn't want him to think that she wasn't there.

But when she peeked through the peephole, it wasn't Noah at all.

"Oh, wow." Shayna stared at the large bouquet of flowers. Noah had sent her an incredible assortment of her favorite flowers: peach tea roses, pink stargazer lilies and purple tulips.

She took the arrangement from the deliveryman, thanked him and then brought the flowers inside.

"I can't believe he thought to do this." She set the crystal vase down gently on the island counter, smelled the fragrance of each type of flower and then took the card out of the plastic holder.

Her face felt flushed with pleasure and surprise as she took the card out of the envelope. She read the writing on the card. "Thinking of you."

But her voice trailed off when she read the name on the card. "Blake."

Shayna stared at that name for a very long time before she put the card back into the envelope and put the envelope in a drawer where she kept her mail. She actually felt a bit sick to her stomach realizing that she had assigned this romantic gesture so quickly to Noah. Blake was such a wonderful, thoughtful man. Why couldn't she love him the way she loved Noah?

Her excitement for her date with Noah a bit dampened, Shayna returned to the task of fixing her hair. By the time she was done, her hair was loose, shiny and falling in soft curls down her back. Overall, she was very pleased with her appearance and hoped that Noah felt the same way.

Noah was always late, but, to her pleasant surprise, he rang the doorbell ten minutes before the time they had agreed upon.

She took a deep breath that did nothing to calm the butterflies in her stomach; she opened the door to find Noah, clean-shaven in black slacks and a light blue button-down shirt that made his eyes look as blue as the ocean waters.

The appreciation that she saw in his eyes let her know that she had made the right choice in her outfit.

"Shayna." Noah's eyes took her in. "You're a knock-out."

"So are you."

Noah stepped inside her house, and she was glad that she had moved Blake's flowers from the kitchen to her art studio. She didn't want anything to detract from her first date with the man who had held her heart since they were just kids.

"Let me just grab my purse."

Noah waited at the door for her, his stance strong and straight; he looked every bit the marine even when he was in civilian clothes. She found that to be incredibly appealing—she really liked this grown-up Noah.

Her clutch in hand, she joined Noah at the door.

"Ready," she said.

"As am I," Noah said, and she felt that there was a distinct undertone in that short phrase. In her mind, Noah was saying that he was ready for their date, yes, but he was also telling her that he was ready for their relationship to deepen. Perhaps she had read too much into his words, but as she took his offered arm and they walked in unison to his truck, Shayna hoped beyond hope that she hadn't read the intention behind his words wrong.

Noah helped her into the truck, shut the door behind her, trotted around the front of the truck and then got behind the wheel.

Shayna smoothed the skirt of her dress, wiping the thin sheen of sweat on her palms dry on the material. Noah slipped the key in the ignition and turned on the truck, but he didn't immediately shift into Reverse. Instead, he looked over at her, an inscrutable expression on his face.

His gaze made her feel self-conscious. She felt her cheeks flush and ran her hand nervously over her hair.

"What?" she finally asked, her anxiety making her simple question sound irritated.

"Nothing," he said, his voice silky smooth with a suggestive undertone. "Everything."

He took her hand in his and kissed it. Then he locked eyes with her and held it.

"You are the most beautiful woman I have ever seen, Shayna," Noah said. "Thank you for agreeing to be my date."

"Thank you, Noah." This was all she could think to say, because her brain felt completely scrambled by his words.

He gave her hand one more kiss, and then he shifted into Reverse.

"Where are you taking me?" she asked, feeling like she needed to make small talk with a man she usually enjoyed long, comfortable silences with.

He smiled a mischievous smile. "That, my love, is a surprise."

Chapter Eleven

Noah couldn't remember the last time he felt nervous about a first date. With Shayna, he felt unsteady, off balance and, honestly, a bit afraid of how the night would unfold. He knew her well enough to know that she would be hypersensitive to any missteps on his part. Was that fair? Maybe not. But his track record was her guide, and he didn't have anyone to blame for his past errors but himself.

"Are we going to Sugar Creek?" Shayna asked him, sounding surprised and concerned.

"Don't worry," he said. "I haven't invited my entire family to our first date."

"Oh, thank goodness."

Her response, so quick and relieved, made him laugh.

"Not that I don't love your family," she added.

"I love them, too," he agreed. "But this night is for us and us alone."

Noah pulled into the drive to his family's ranch and then took the first right down a rustic road carved into the Montana landscape. He drove through a lush tree canopy that eventually opened up to a clearing with a log cabin, several equipment barns and a horse stable.

"Isn't this Liam's place?" Shayna asked.

"Yes." Noah parked the truck right in front of the cabin and shut off the engine. "I hope you aren't disappointed."

Her brow was a bit wrinkled, and he did see disappointment on her face. He imagined Shayna felt that she had put on her pretty dress to go out in Bozeman, and now he was taking her to a cabin in the woods instead.

His date didn't respond for several seconds, and then she asked bluntly. "You aren't trying to hide me away, are you?"

Those words hit Noah in the gut like he'd been sucker punched. That thought would have never crossed his mind. He turned toward her so she could get a good look at his face; he wanted her to see the truth in his eyes.

"I would never hide you away, Shayna." He tried his best to reassure her. "I have given a lot of thought to this first date, and I just need you to go along for the ride just a little while longer."

She looked at the cabin and then looked at him.

He prompted her, "Do you trust me?"

Her hesitance didn't surprise him. Noah knew he

had a long way to go to build trust with Shayna as her lover and partner.

"I do trust you, Noah," Shayna finally said.

He rewarded her with a smile. "Good! That's good!"

He jumped out of the truck, jogged around to her side and then opened the door for her. She climbed out, and he could tell that she was trying not to ruin her shoes as the heels began to sink into the grass and dirt.

Noah bent down, scooped her up and swung her into his arms.

Shayna made the sweetest shocked noise that was music to his ears.

"Noah!" she exclaimed, wrapping her arms around his neck. "No. I'm too heavy."

"You're light as a feather to me." Noah ignored her protests and easily carried her up the steps of the cabin and put her down gently.

Shayna's cheeks were flushed, her green eyes shining with a mix of happy emotions.

"I didn't want you to ruin your shoes," he said as he went back to the truck, grabbed her purse from the passenger seat and then shut the door.

"You're crazy." She laughed at him, looking absolutely delectable to him. It was the rawness of the setting juxtaposed with how stunning and classy she looked in that dress that showed off her curves in the most appealing way.

"I'm crazy about you," he said easily. And he knew, without one doubt, that he meant it. Shayna had been right in front of his eyes for nearly his entire life, and now he was man enough to see it.

"Close your eyes," he said, his hand on the doorknob.

Shayna covered her eyes; he was glad to see the smile on her face when he guided her through the open doorway.

Just as he had planned, Shayna's favorite classical music pieces were playing gently in the background. It was exactly what Noah had wanted to set the mood.

"Is that Puccini?" Shayna asked, and he heard the breathiness in her voice. His surprise, one of many planned, had worked.

"Yes." Noah closed the door behind them. "It is."

Along with the music, Noah knew that Shayna's senses would also detect the fragrance of Italian food being cooked in the quaint kitchen. Liam's cabin was small, with a pitched roof in the living room and dark, stained wood as the main construction material. This cabin had brought several of his brothers luck—Liam, Shane and Hunter had all made connections with their wives in this secluded, private oasis. If he executed his plan and was blessed with a dash of luck, Noah would be making his own connection with his future wife.

"Open your eyes," Noah instructed.

Shayna slowly opened her eyes, and he watched her face, wanting to take in every emotion that crossed her pretty face.

"Oh, Noah," she whispered. "You did all of this for me?"

"Of course." He put his arm around her waist. "Dr. Shayna Wade, I'd like to introduce you to Chef Mason."

Noah had hired a private chef to cook all of Shayna's favorite Italian foods. Every menu selection, from the appetizers to the desserts, had been made with her in mind.

"Good evening, Dr. Wade," the chef said formally. "Dinner will be served shortly."

Shayna looked up at him with wonder on her face. "It's all so beautiful, Noah."

He had tried to think of everything. He had asked Lee, Colt's wife and Shayna's best friend, to help him with the decorative details. Lee had been willing to help, but he also sensed that she was worried about Shayna's heart. Noah knew that with most people—including his own family—he was going to have to prove his worthiness as Shayna's partner over time. He knew that he was ready to hang up his international playboy hat—it would just take time and patience for the rest of the world to recognize the change in him. In his mind, Shayna was the one who truly mattered. If she believed in him, then he was the winner.

"How did you do all of this?" she asked as he pulled out her seat at the table for two that was positioned in the center of the living room to take advantage of the glorious views.

"I had some help," he admitted with a secretive smile as he took his seat across from her. "We will be able to see the sun set behind the mountain."

Chef Mason brought over a bottle of Shayna's favorite chianti.

"May I pour you a glass of wine?" the chef asked.

"Absolutely." Shayna said and, to him, she seemed more relaxed now than she had when he had picked her up. Her ease was helping him feel less nervous.

"Here's to you." He held up his glass.

"Here's to us," Shayna corrected before she touched her glass to his.

"To us," he agreed.

After he drank some of the wine, he reached over to take her free hand in his. "I know you were disappointed that we didn't go into town."

He played with her fingers, liking the way her hand fit in his. "Are you still disappointed?"

She put down her glass and put her other hand over his. "I've never had anyone do this for me, Noah. This is the most romantic moment of my life."

"Mission accomplished, then." Pleased, he sat a little straighter in his chair. "Because that's exactly what I was aiming for."

Noah had wanted to ensure that he had planned the best first date Shayna had ever had by miles; he wanted to make sure that no man in her past could touch him. And from the dreamy expression on Shayna's face, he'd succeeded.

In between courses, the chef discreetly went outside to allow them the privacy Noah had been after in the first place. The wine and good food had loosened them both up, and it seemed to him that they were back to being themselves—relaxed, laughing and smiling—but with a little extra spice. Now when he looked across the table at his best friend, he found his mind returning again and again to the kiss good night. Those lips—those soft, sweet, enticing lips—had never seemed more kissable.

"I am so full." Shayna laughed, her hands on her stomach. "I'm going to have to take it easy on the calories this week, that's for sure."

Noah cut a piece of lemon ricotta cake and held it out for her to taste. "Just take a bite and we can save the rest for later."

Shayna took the bite from his fork, closed her eyes in delight and made a pleasurable sound in the back of her throat.

"Mmm." She opened her eyes. "That is amazing."

He took a bite as well and then put down his fork. As if sensing that they were ready for him to clear dessert and offer them a strong cup of coffee, Chef Mason appeared and quickly cleared the table.

"Let's take our coffee out on the porch and watch the sunset," Noah suggested.

Shayna held her cup carefully and nodded her agreement.

Outside on the porch, they both sat down in the creaky rocking chairs, and Shayna bent down to unhook the buckles on her strappy shoes. When she bent over, Noah was treated to a glance at her deep cleavage. Noah knew good and well that he needed to take it slow with Shayna. He couldn't rush her into bed no matter how much he wanted to make love to her. And God, did he want to make love to her. Again and again until they both drifted off into a satisfied sleep.

Chef Mason quickly cleaned up the kitchen and dishes, packed the tools of his trade, and slipped by them on the porch. The chef had parked behind the cabin in order to hide that anyone was awaiting them inside. Noah was very satisfied with how his plan had been executed. In his mind, this was the best first date for both of them.

"This has been the most incredible night, Noah." Shayna had her bare feet propped up on the railing; the hem of her dress had shimmied up to midthigh. Her skin looked so buttery soft that his fingers ached to explore her body. It would be so easy to slip his hand under that slinky little dress and touch her in a way that would have her closing her eyes, licking her lips and begging him to join their bodies together so he could give her a release she would never forget. It wouldn't be tonight—but he couldn't imagine leaving Montana without having made love to Shayna. Part of him felt it was important to shatter that platonic barrier in order to close the door permanently on Shayna's flirtation with Blake Foreman. Shayna would never make love to him and then fall into the arms of another man. That kind of behavior had never been in her nature.

"You deserve it," he said.

She reached over to take his hand in hers. "I was nervous. About tonight. About how it would feel."

"So was I." He threaded their fingers together. "That's

why I chose this spot. So we could have privacy." He kissed the back of her hand. "But we did okay, didn't we?"

He saw her swallow hard several times. "So far."

Noah heard the worry in her voice, and he didn't like it. He sat up, turning his chair so he was facing in her direction. "I wish you didn't have doubts about me."

"Noah," she said kindly, "you have to give me a minute to…process all of this. This is new to me. And I know you feel a sense of urgency because your time in the States is so short…" She took her feet down from the railing in order to sit upright. "And I worry…"

"About what?"

Shayna breathed in, and he could tell from years of knowing her that she was trying to find the right words—she was afraid that she was going to hurt him.

"I'm worried that you haven't really thought about the risk."

"What risk?"

"If this doesn't work, Noah."

"It will work."

"But if it *doesn't* work, Noah—" She had been averting her eyes until she said these next words. "Our friendship will be ruined."

Her stark assessment took the smile right off his face. "I can't believe that."

"But you have to believe it, Noah, because it's true. I can't go down this road with you, invest my heart and then, if it doesn't work…"

"Because I screwed it up…"

"Not necessarily," she denied, but it was a weak denial and they both knew it. "It takes two people to make something work, and it takes two to make it fail."

Noah leaned forward; he clasped both her hands between his. "Could you do me a favor, Shay?"

She nodded.

"Don't doubt us before we've even had a chance to try."

He saw that his words had hit their intended mark. Noah let go of her hands in order to grab the arms of her rocking chair and pull her, chair and all, close enough so he could easily reach her lips. He ran his fingers through her soft, shiny hair and pressed his lips to hers. She was ready for his kisses; her intake of breath was the perfect time to deepen the kiss. She tasted like red wine and lemon, and they kissed each other while the sun set on the horizon and the sweet Montana evening air sent a chill through Shayna's body.

"Cold?" he asked her.

When she nodded, he sat back and opened his arms, inviting her to sit on his lap. "Come over here, my love. I'll keep you warm."

It was a starry night, and Shayna felt satiated and sleepy on the drive home. She leaned back her seat and closed her eyes. Noah reached over to hold her hand; how often had she dreamed of a moment like this? A simple, routine act that she had seen couples do for so many years—holding hands on the way home after a wonderful date. Now it was her turn with Noah.

"I'm going to see May tomorrow." Noah's words brought her out of the downward drift toward sleep.

"Is there anything new?"

"I checked on her before I picked you up. She's well enough to return to the rehab center."

"Oh, thank goodness." Shayna turned her head to look at Noah's profile in the dim light. "I know Isabella has been missing her."

"I'll take her to see May the day after tomorrow," he said. "I also have a meeting with my commander to extend my leave."

"That's good."

"And I have an appointment with my attorney."

"A big day."

"A very big day."

Shayna yawned loudly as Noah pulled into her driveway. "Oh my Lord. You've done me in, Noah."

"I'll see you in."

She nodded, opened her door instead of waiting for him to come around to her side and wobbled a bit, still woozy from the wine, on her way to the front door. Noah met her at the walkway and offered her his arm.

"What a handsome man you are, Noah."

"What a beautiful woman you are, Shayna."

"Hmm."

"Are you tipsy?" he asked her.

"Totally."

Shayna attempted to get the key in the lock; after a few misfires, Noah took her keys and opened the door.

"Show-off," she teased him.

Noah hung her keys on the hook near the door. Pilot creaked and cracked his way over to them with a slow wag of his tail.

"Oh, my handsome boy." Shayna kissed the dog on his head. "You must be about ready to burst."

"As am I," Noah piped up.

"Well, go take care of that, sir." She waved her hand toward the bathroom down the hall. "I'm going to take Pilot out, poor baby."

Over her shoulder, she said, "Come find me when you're done."

Noah handled his business and then went out into the backyard, where he found Shayna lying flat on her back in the plush grass.

"Dr. Wade?"

"Hmm?"

"May I have this dance?"

"There isn't any music."

"I can fix that." He held out his hands for her.

Her laugh sounded like a lilting wind chime; she reached up her hands to let him pull her up. Then he did a quick search on his phone for the one song that reminded him of Shayna and hit Play.

He opened his arms, and Shayna melted into his body, her arms around his neck, the fragrance of her hair and the softness of her skin tantalizing his senses.

"Perfect," she murmured, her head tucked under his chin.

"This is perfect."

"No." She laughed again. "The song. Every time I hear this song, I think of us."

"Me, too," he said, tightening his hold on her waist.

Beneath the dark sky dotted with clusters of brilliant, twinkling stars, Noah kissed Shayna, on her lips, on her neck, until he was noticeably aroused. He knew Shayna could feel the way his body was responding to having her in his arms; he wanted her to feel it—to know without a doubt that he desired her.

"Let's go inside." She had a sultry, well-kissed resonance in her voice.

She had a hold on his hand as she led him back inside. They walked past the bed and went into the main living room to the couch. He sat down, and she immediately curled herself into his body.

"Hmm." She sighed, her eyes closed. "You smell so good."

"So do you." He pulled her closer.

It had been years since he sat on a couch with a woman; it reminded him of being a kid, sitting on the couch, in the dark, in May's house, trying to get to second base with Annika. As soon as Isabella's mother came into his mind, he pushed her image aside. This night was for Shayna, no one else.

He couldn't seem to stop kissing her, and soon they were lying together facing each other on the couch, making out like they were teenagers. He wanted to be respectful—he needed to be respectful—but when Shayna pressed her body against his and wound her leg suggestively over his, Noah found his hand on her full, soft breast, and he kissed the curve. Her hands were around his neck, her head was tilted back, her breathing was shallow and she was making these sexy little moans that were driving him crazy.

"We should stop." Noah couldn't believe he was actually saying those words.

"Okay," she agreed, but her body was still searching for his.

Noah forced himself to sit up and brought her with him. He fixed her dress, pulling the front of her dress over to cover her semiexposed breast. Then he tugged at his pants to release some of the pressure from his groin.

"Damn, Shayna." Noah ran his hands through his hair several times. "Damn."

"I thought it would be…awkward," she said, her chest still rising and falling in a way that made him want to abandon his resolve and strip her out of that hot little dress and give her everything her body was asking for.

"It's far from awkward."

In fact, it felt more natural with Shayna than it had with any other woman. She felt like home to him—the way she smelled, the way she tasted, the sensual curves of her body.

"I'd better go home."

"You should go home."

Noah stood up and held out his hand for her.

"Before you go, let me grab a card that I bought for May."

"That was sweet of you," he said, feeling ridiculous standing in Shayna's living room with a raging hard-on.

While Shayna went to her bedroom to get the card out of her everyday purse, Noah wandered into her art studio. There, on the small café table, was a large bouquet of flowers. The flowers were fresh—and they weren't from him.

The card wasn't with the flowers, but Noah already knew that they were a gift from Blake. Perhaps he had been overconfident in Shayna's feelings for him. It hadn't even occurred to him that Foreman was still a thing after he had declared his love for her. Now, looking at this flower arrangement, Noah began to wonder just how exclusive Shayna intended to be. For him, it was an all-or-nothing deal. Maybe that wasn't fair, and maybe he didn't really have the right, but that was the way it had to be.

"Noah?" Shayna called out his name when she didn't find him in the living room.

"In here."

Shayna was still feeling like she was floating across the floor after her epic first date with the man of her dreams. In fact, she was still so fuzzy-brained between the endorphins and red wine that she hadn't even remembered the flowers that Blake had sent to her earlier that day. And by the time she *did* remember, she was standing next to Noah staring at them.

"Oh," she said. "Noah, I completely forgot about these."

Noah had his hands in his pockets—she could see

that he wasn't pleased with his discovery. When Noah was upset, he went inside himself like a turtle retreating into its shell.

"Foreman?"

"Yes."

Noah didn't look at her; he was still looking at the flowers. "When are you going to tell him?"

"Tomorrow. Of course, I will tell him tomorrow."

Noah's body was stiff, his mouth thin. After a silence between them, Noah said in a monotone voice, "I'm not playing a game here, Shayna."

Shayna wrapped her arms around Noah's waist and held on to him. After a moment, he returned her hug.

"This isn't a game for me, either, Noah. I'm putting everything on the line," she said. "My heart, my future. Everything."

He rested his chin on her head, a move that reassured her as she was trying to reassure him.

"Am I your future, Shayna?" Noah asked her quietly, seriously.

"Noah." She rested her head over his strong heart. "You are my past, my present and my future."

"I love you, Dr. Wade."

Shayna tilted her head back so he could kiss her. How she dearly loved Noah's kisses.

"And I love you, Captain Brand."

Chapter Twelve

"I'm sorry, Blake." Shayna had asked Blake to meet her in the park where they regularly worked out together the next day.

The handsome trainer sat next to her quietly, but she could see in his face and eyes that he was disappointed.

"I thought something was up when you didn't call to thank me for the flowers."

She cringed inside. It wasn't her nature to leave a gift unacknowledged. Her only excuse, flimsy as it was, was that she'd been completely focused on getting ready for her long-awaited date with Noah.

"I am sorry, Blake. Really, I am. It was so rude of me to not at least text."

He gave her the briefest of smiles. "My timing wasn't so good."

She put her hand on his arm. "You are such a wonderful man, Blake. We've always been friends. I hope that won't change."

"Of course it won't," he assured her. "Actually, we really haven't moved passed friendship, I don't think. Not really. In the back of my mind, I think I knew that you weren't over Brand."

She put her hands in her lap. "I don't think I'll ever really be over him."

"At least now," the trainer said, "maybe you won't have to."

She nodded but didn't put words to her thoughts. The night before with Noah had seemed like a dream. After he left, her body had been charged with desire, sexual frustration and blatant need for his touch. It had taken every ounce of her willpower not to rip his clothes off and just let the consequences be damned. But, luckily for her, they both had managed to exercise some caution in that area. Now, in the light of day, Shayna felt unsteady and unsure, two feelings she didn't like at all. Yes, Noah had planned an incredibly romantic first date that any woman would love. And she *had* loved it. Yet, that didn't inspire confidence in his feelings for her. And, surprisingly, her heart and her mind were not as open to Noah as they once were. In the past, she would have leaped into his arms without looking twice. Now, her approach to Noah was much warier and more jaded. She wasn't the doe-eyed young girl she had been, and she couldn't go back to that person even if she wanted to.

"Will you still be coming to me for training?" Blake asked her.

"I hope so!" Shayna said with an exclamation point in her voice. "I still want to. Do you?"

"How will Noah feel about that?"

Shayna frowned at the question. "I haven't asked him. It's not his decision."

Blake was about to ask her another question when her cell phone rang. "I need to take this."

"Go ahead."

She stood up and walked a few feet away. "Hi."

"Hi, my love," Noah said.

It still sounded odd to her ears that he had started to call her *my love*. He had always just called her Shay, and it didn't feel, at least not yet, that she was this *my love* person.

"Hi," she said, this time with a smile in her voice.

"Where are you?"

"I'm with Blake at the park."

Noah was silent for a second or two before he asked, "Can you meet me at your house? I need to talk to you."

"When?"

"Fifteen minutes?"

"Okay," she agreed. "I'll see you there."

Noah wasn't one for urgent talks, so there had to be something awfully important for him to call. She ended the call and turned back to Blake.

"I have to go."

He stood up with a nod. "I figured."

"Can we meet next week for a training session?" she asked. "I don't want to lose my momentum."

"That's what I want to hear," her trainer said. "I'll see you next week."

Blake held out his hand for her to shake, but she bypassed his hand and hugged him. "Thank you, Blake. For the flowers, the advice, the training."

She looked up at him. "And for wanting to take me out on dates."

Blake's eyes touched on the features of her face as if he were trying to memorize them. "Don't ever forget how special you are, Shayna."

"I'll try my best."

"And don't let Brand ever forget it, either."

Noah arrived at Shayna's house first and waited for her in the driveway. He hadn't liked the fact that she was with Blake so soon after their first date, but Shayna wasn't an overly jealous person, and she certainly didn't like it in other people. They hadn't discussed it, but Noah was pretty positive that she was going to keep right on training with Foreman even though the man had designs on her that went beyond a trainer-client relationship.

Noah hopped out of his truck when he saw Shayna's mint-condition muscle car turning into the driveway. She rolled her window down and smiled at him with such love and happiness to see him that the jealousy he had been trying to suppress dissipated like fog in sunlight. It just vanished.

"Let me just put this in the garage," she said.

He was so anxious to get her back in his arms that he followed behind her on foot and was there to open her door when she shut off the engine.

"Good morning." He held out his hand for her, and she smiled at him again, a bit shyly this time, and took his offered hand.

"It's almost afternoon," she said.

Noah pulled her into his arms, lowered his head and whispered, "Then, good afternoon."

He kissed her several times before he let her go. "I've been missing that."

She linked her arm with his, and he enjoyed seeing the pretty blush on her neck and her cheeks. His kisses made her blush, and *that* fact made him feel like another of his missions had been accomplished.

"How did it go with Foreman?" he asked directly on their way to her front door.

"I didn't want to hurt him," she admitted. "He's a wonderful man. He really is."

"He's just not the man for you."

She met his gaze, and in those bright green eyes he saw her soul so clearly. "No. He's not."

"Because that's my job." Noah felt the need to reiterate this fact to her. Perhaps because he could still sense doubt in her. She was still grappling with what seemed to her like a sudden shift in his feelings for her. But he hadn't experienced it that way at all. Yes, the realization *had* hit him over the head like a cartoon who had been struck with a mallet. On the other hand, he had been looking at her social media feeds for months, and he had been missing Shayna—missing the feeling of home whenever he was with her. So, in his mind, he had been falling in love with her for a while without even realizing it.

She opened the door. "I hope so."

"Don't hope." He closed the door behind them. *"Know."*

Shayna offered him a drink, and then they took Pilot out for his umpteenth bathroom break of the day. There were dark clouds in the sky and a mugginess in the air that was a precursor to storms later in the day.

"Do you want to sit in the gazebo?" Shayna had kicked off her shoes and was barefoot in the grass.

"It seems like we always have our serious talks there."

She glanced over at him. "Is this good news or bad news?"

"Good," he said. "All good."

Side by side, their arms and legs touching, they sat on the gazebo bench. Noah noted that it was the same spot they had occupied together the night he had arrived in Bozeman a few short weeks ago.

Noah slipped a folded envelope out of his shirt pocket and handed it to her.

Shayna put her glass of sweet tea on the bench next to her, opened the envelope and unfolded the piece of paper inside. She scanned it, and once she realized what she was looking at, Noah saw, as he'd hoped he would see, an expression of sheer joy.

"Oh, Noah."

"I wanted you to be the first person I told."

Shayna turned toward him and hugged him tightly. "She's yours."

"She's ours," he corrected.

Getting the results of the paternity test had been slow as getting molasses out of a bottle. COVID-19 had seemed to jam a lot of gears. But now that he had the results, he could petition the courts for temporary custody and establish child support for May when she got better. He didn't think it made sense to turn Isabella's world upside down; eventually, Noah had every intention of at least being awarded joint custody. He had already missed too many years with his daughter; he wasn't going to let anyone—not Annika and not May— rob him of any more time with Isabella.

Shayna handed the envelope back to him. "I'm so happy for you."

Noah rested his arm comfortably around Shayna's shoulders. "I'm happy for *us*."

It didn't go unnoticed by him that he had to keep correcting her. It was if she was already trying to put distance between them with her words.

"I have more news."

She looked at him and waited.

"My hardship leave has been extended."

That brought an expression of surprise and happiness to her pretty, naturally lovely face.

"Are you serious?"

"Yes."

"Thank goodness!" she said with a relieved sigh. "I was so worried about what was going to happen if you had to leave next week! Especially since May isn't near ready to go home."

"My commander is a good guy. He's always had my back. Now I've got some extra time to get things in order here." Noah kissed her on the top of Shayna's head. "And I have some extra time to spend with you."

Shayna rewarded his words by snuggling a bit closer to him. Their silence was comfortable—it always had been, and Noah believed that it always would be. Yes, their relationship had evolved, and there would be rough waters to navigate ahead. But this wasn't a new relationship—they had a long history and knew each other's stories. Unlike most new couples, they already had the getting-to-know-you phase out of the way. They were best friends, and soon, Noah hoped, they would be lovers as well.

Noah held Shayna closely, his mind whirling with ideas and plans. He could imagine a time when they were married and Isabella was living with them. They could be a family, the three of them. It wasn't how he had imagined it when he was a younger man—but, truth be told, it was *better*, because he would be making a family with Shayna.

A couple of fat raindrops hit the roof of the gazebo, interrupting his daydreaming.

"It's starting to rain." Shayna jumped up like a jack-in-the-box. "Pilot hates the rain!"

Together, hand in hand, they ran across the yard like two overgrown kids, trying to dodge raindrops. They reached the back porch of the house, laughing at their own silliness. Pilot was slowly climbing the steps, shaking his head every time a drop of rain landed on it.

"Come on, Pilot!" they encouraged him. "You can do it!"

Together, the three of them went back inside, and Shayna grabbed a towel out of her bathroom to rub over Pilot's damp fur.

"There you go, old man." Shayna hugged the Great Dane fondly before she threw the dirty towel in the hamper.

"Are you hungry?" she asked over her shoulder.

"Starving." He followed her into the kitchen and sat on one of the bar stools.

Shayna gathered items from the fridge to make a salad. He knew how important her lifestyle change was to her, and he wanted to be supportive. If she wanted to eat salad six nights a week and have one cheat day, he was going to prove that Foreman wasn't the only man around who cared about her health.

"What kind of salad dressing?" she asked.

"Whatever you're having."

"Oil and vinegar."

"Sounds good."

Noah was beginning to feel, now that many of the pieces were on the board, that his path forward was clearer, and he was starting to feel like he was standing on more solid ground. He had managed to convince Shayna to give a relationship with him a shot, he now had proof that Isabella was his flesh and blood, and now his leave had been extended. For most of his life he had sought excitement and change; it came as a bit of a surprise that what really mattered to him, what he really enjoyed, was the quiet moments that he spent with Shayna, whether it was eating a salad or watching the sun set.

"Are you finished?" Shayna asked, taking her bowl to the sink.

"It was good, thank you."

He came around to the sink and scooted her out of his way. "You fixed the salads, I'll rinse the bowls."

"Are you serious, Captain Brand?"

He winked at her. "I'm capable of growing."

"I love a man who has some domestic skills," Shayna teased him. "I'll just wait for you right over here on the couch."

Once he was finished with the dishes, he joined her on the sofa. She curled her body into his with her knees pulled up and a bit flopped over onto his leg.

"So what other domestic skills have you developed?"

"I can vacuum."

"Amazing."

"Iron."

"Iron?" She widened her eyes. "Amazing."

"And if it's something you're interested in, I could,

just for you, cook for you in nothing but my Kiss the Cook apron."

"Now, that is something I'd be interested in." She leaned her head back on the arm that was wrapped around her shoulders.

"Would you like a preview?" he asked.

"Please."

Noah dropped soft, sweet butterfly kisses on her lips that made her smile with pleasure.

"What are you going to do today?" he asked her.

"Working on research for my book and meeting with some of the students about the Christmas display."

"I was hoping you'd be able to come with Isabella and me to see May."

"I wish I could," she said. "But I think it's good for you to have some one-on-one time with your daughter."

They kissed for several more minutes, necking on the couch like two high school kids.

"I have to go," he said against her lips.

"I know."

"Call you later?"

"Call me later."

"Oh, my sweet baby!" May exclaimed in a scratchy, weak voice. "I'm so glad to see you."

Isabella ran over to her grandmother and leaped onto the bed. "Nanna! Where have you been?"

"Be careful, Isabella," Noah warned the little girl.

"Oh, she's just as right as rain," May said, hugging Isabella as tightly as she could.

"I wanted to come see you," Isabella told her grandmother as if she were tattling.

"I know you did, bug." May ran her hand over the little girl's ponytail. "It's been a lot of work getting better so we can go home."

"Can we go home today?"

"Not today, sweet-sweet." May held Isabella by her side as if she was afraid to let go of her. "But soon."

Isabella frowned, and then she started to cry. "I want to go home, Nanna. I want to go home."

"Aren't you having a good time at Sugar Creek? I've seen pictures of you riding them horses like a regular cowgirl."

"I suppose." Isabella sniffed loudly.

"Now, we'll have no tears." May wiped Isabella's face with tissues that Noah had handed her. "You're a big girl getting ready for first grade."

"I have to get all of my stuff for school," Isabella reminded her grandmother anxiously. "New clothes, a new book bag, pencils, crayons…"

"I haven't forgotten," May said, her voice sounding weaker after a short conversation.

"I'll make sure you're ready for school, Isabella." Noah sat down in a chair near the window.

"But Nanna does that for me!" she told him. "That's *her* job, not *yours*."

"Isabella." May put her shaking hand on her granddaughter's face. "If I ask Noah to help you, I want you to promise me that you will show him what a big girl you are. He's never gotten anyone ready for school before, so he'll need your help."

Isabella did not seem at all willing to give up on her nanna helping her; instead of answering, she clammed up and refused to answer.

"Promise?" May tickled her neck.

"Okay, Nanna." Isabella laughed at being tickled. "But I probably won't have to, 'cause you'll be better by then."

May looked over the child's head to meet Noah's gaze. There was something hollow in May's weary eyes—something odd that he couldn't quite put his finger on.

"That's true," May said to Isabella. "I bet I will be better by then."

They visited for another hour, and then May's voice gave out, her face went white and her hands were shaking so badly that she had to clasp them together.

"I love you, Nanna." Isabella hugged her one last time, and Noah knew that she didn't want to let go.

"I love you, sweet-sweet." May reached out with her unsteady hand and touched her granddaughter's cheek. "Always remember, I love you to the moon and back."

"And all around the world and back," Isabella said.

"Yes, my darling girl," May said in a breathy voice. "All around the world and back."

Shayna believed that she would look back on the two weeks she spent with Noah and Isabella setting up her Christmas village as some of the most precious memories of her life. Noah had painted the shelves, and he had even had a friend who owned Bozeman Electric come and install discreet outlets along the length of the shelves so Shayna wouldn't have to run unsightly extension cords in order to bring the village to life.

"How's this?" Noah was on a ladder working to place the carousel on the shelf in a way that would earn the approval of Shayna's critical eye.

"Just one more inch to the left."

Noah eyeballed an inch and moved it. "How 'bout now?"

"Um." Shayna's eyes were slightly narrowed in thought. "I don't know. Something is off."

"Shay! You've had me moving this carousel back and forth for the last half hour."

"It needs to be perfect."

"I think it was perfect a half hour ago," Noah grumbled.

Shayna was not affected by his grumbling at all. Installing her village was like putting a puzzle together—every piece had to fit perfectly in order for the picture to be complete.

"If you were down here, you would see what I'm seeing."

"The last time I *was* down there, I loved it. And then you moved it ten more times."

Shayna was just about to serve another verbal volley to Noah when the doorbell rang. "Saved by the bell."

"Thank God." Noah climbed down from the ladder.

"I'm going to get a beer. You're driving me to drink, woman."

Shayna walked toward the door, but she tossed over her shoulder, "I'm making the perfect Christmas, Noah. That kind of thing takes time and patience."

She was laughing at Noah's nonstop grumbling when she opened the door.

"Lee!" She hadn't been expecting to see her friend and neighbor standing at her door. "I didn't know you were going to be in the neighborhood today. Come in, come in!"

Lee was carrying her one-year-old son, Junior, in her arms.

"Oh my goodness." Shayna reached for the little boy. "He's a chubby one, isn't he?"

"That boy puts away so much food, you wouldn't believe it. I can't even imagine what it's going to be like when he's a teenager."

Lee greeted Noah, who had found a beer in the fridge, and they all went into the formal living room together.

"You have your village up," Lee said. "It looks great."

Shayna sat down next to Noah and made faces to make Junior laugh; the boy giggled and smiled at her and reached for her ponytail.

"You're such a handsome boy, aren't you?" Shayna used a lilting pitch that caught and held the baby's attention. "He's the spitting image of Colt," she said to her friend.

"I know." Lee sat down in a nearby chair. "Colt

walks around like a strutting peacock, he's so proud. You should see Colt's baby pictures. You'd swear on a Bible that it was Junior."

"Where is Colt?" Noah asked.

"Next door. It took some doing, but I finally got him to agree to move back to the house. He's been happy at Sugar Creek—and I love it, don't get me wrong—but I miss my house. It's set up for me to get around more easily," Lee said and then added about her rotund gray tabby cat, "Chester will be much happier, too."

Lee had had her left leg amputated just above the knee when she was in college; she walked and jogged and rode horses with her advanced prosthetic and lived her life basically like most people. But when she was home, it wasn't always convenient to use the prosthetic, so she used a wheelchair or crutches, and sometimes she got on the ground and scooted.

"It's your home." Shayna nodded her understanding. "And I'm really glad you're moving back. I've missed having you right next door."

"I've missed you." Lee stood up. "I just wanted to pop over for a quick hello. I'd better get back before Colt sends out a search party."

Shayna gave up the baby reluctantly. She kissed his soft, fat cheeks.

"You know—" Lee took her son into her arms "—that carousel isn't centered."

Shayna laughed. "That's exactly what I just told him!"

Noah frowned playfully at his sister-in-law and pointed to the door. "Lee. Out!"

Chapter Thirteen

For the next couple of weeks, Shayna focused on all her projects: research for the book, the Christmas display and painting. She was actually glad that Noah was also busy helping his family at Sugar Creek, taking Isabella shopping for school, visiting May and working with his attorney to make sure his daughter was provided for and cared for. Shayna hadn't considered what it would be like to have a boyfriend in her life again—during the pandemic, it had been lonely, yes, but she also had the freedom to do as she pleased without thinking of anyone else. It sounded selfish, she knew that, but she liked her alone time, and she liked the flexibility that came with being a party of one.

It was late morning in the final days of summer when

Shayna crossed the short distance from her front door to Lee's front door.

"Hi!" Lee had her glossy mahogany hair in a high ponytail. "Junior is taking a nap."

Shayna nodded and walked in quietly. Once in the kitchen, she took a seat at Lee's enormous marble island and took the cup of hot, black coffee that her friend offered.

"You look amazing," Lee said, holding her own cup of piping-hot coffee.

"Thank you." She smiled, pleased. Lee was straightforward and blunt, and she only said what she meant. A person always knew where they stood with Lee.

"So." Lee put her cup down near the baby monitor and leaned her elbows on the countertop, her face expectant. "Spill the beans."

"It's been…" Shayna paused, because she had to think of the right words to say. "It's been weirdly wonderful, if you know what I mean?"

"I think so." Lee rested her hip against the counter with a puzzled expression on her undeniably lovely face.

Shayna held her coffee mug, enjoying the warm feel of it in her hands. "It's Noah—so we know each other's secrets. We know each other's faults. There isn't really any mystery between us."

"Is that a good thing or a bad thing?"

"I don't know, really," she answered honestly. "It's just a *thing*. So, it's not like a brand-new relationship with years of discovery ahead."

Lee continued to look puzzled. Shayna knew why—

Shayna had been madly in love with Noah for almost her entire life, and now that she finally had her heart's desire, she wasn't over the moon with giddiness.

"Have the two of you…?" Lee raised her eyebrows suggestively.

Shayna shook her head. "We've made out like high school kids."

"And," her friend asked, "how was that?"

"Good."

"Oh." Lee sounded disappointed. "No fireworks?"

"Well, I love to snuggle with him. But, then again, I've always liked to do that." Shayna hadn't really analyzed it before now. "And I like to hold his hand, but then again—"

"You've always liked to do that."

Shayna nodded. "My body does light up like a Christmas tree when he kisses me."

"That's something!"

"He really is a great kisser." She felt as if she needed to defend Noah's honor for some strange reason. "And he is so incredibly handsome."

Lee nodded. "The Brand men are hot."

"Totally," Shayna agreed. "But the idea of Noah— my best friend—seeing me naked… In theory I don't mind at all. I'm proud of my body—I like how I look and how I feel."

"I sense another but coming,"

"But it's *Noah*," she said. "I've always fantasized about him, but the reality is so different. I can't seem to cross that line with him."

"And how does he feel about it?" Lee topped off her coffee. "Have you talked to him?"

"No. I mean, we've both said that we're going to take it slow."

Lee examined her with a keen eye. "Shayna, we've known each other for a long time. I think we know each other pretty well. I think you're scared to cross that line with him because you know there isn't any going back once you do."

Shayna took a sip of her coffee and mulled over the truth in Lee's words. She was right, of course. Once they made love, the friendship they had built over decades would be lost if the romantic relationship failed.

"I do think you're right about that," she said. "I also think it's a matter of trust."

Lee nodded her understanding. "You're still not sure that Noah is in this for the long haul."

"Right." Shayna nodded. "It's still hard for me to believe that *all of a sudden* Noah is in love with me. It just doesn't make logical sense."

Lee came around the counter and sat on a stool next to her. "You know, when Noah came to me to ask for my help planning your first date…"

"Thank you for that, by the way."

"I was happy to do it." Lee said. "But I have to tell you, I was super skeptical of whether or not Noah was sincere about his feelings for you. Not that I thought he was aware of it, but I did wonder whether or not it wasn't a response to the fact that his world had just been rocked by suddenly becoming a father—" Lee snapped her fingers "—just like that."

"I know. Me, too."

"But—" Lee leaned her arm on the counter "—I tell you, Shayna, I've never seen Noah like this before. He means it. He's in love with you."

Shayna sat silent and listened to her friend's words. It seemed to her that this was exactly what she needed to hear—an outsider's perspective.

Lee added, "You know I would be the first one to sound the alarm if I saw any red flags with Noah. I just don't."

Shayna felt excited—and scared—energy coursing through her body. Lee had a way of reading people that was uncanny and she believed that Noah's feelings were sincere. Perhaps this wasn't just an overreaction to the discovery of his daughter. Perhaps Noah really *did* love her the way she had always wanted him to love her—with his whole body, mind, heart and soul.

"That doesn't mean that he doesn't need to earn your trust. That doesn't even mean that he won't screw things up royally. But if you're worried that he doesn't have true feelings for you, I think you can cross that off your list. The man's in love with you, Shayna."

Just as Lee finished her point, Chester the cat walked in, raised his tail and gave one meow before he flopped down onto his side and began to purr happily. Chester was as big as a medium-size dog.

"Lee," Shayna said, "what in the world are you feeding this cat?"

Lee's brow wrinkled. "He's on a diet."

"Really?" Shayna replied. "Most diets entail *losing* weight."

"Don't listen to her, Chester." Lee talked sweetly to her beloved cat. "You're just big boned, that's all."

Shayna visited with Lee until baby Junior awakened from his nap. She spent a little bit of time making a fuss over Lee and Colt's son before she headed back to her house. She was about to head back inside when Noah pulled into her driveway with Isabella sitting in the back seat.

"Hi!" She waved, happy to see them both. "What have you been up to?"

Noah looked frazzled and frustrated. "Clothes shopping."

Isabella hopped out of the truck, ran over to her and gave her a big hug. It had taken some time for her to bond with Isabella, but they had forged a relationship based on their shared love of painting, Christmas, unicorns and Pilot.

"Did you have a good time?" she asked Isabella.

"No."

"No?"

Isabella shook her head. "Noah doesn't know how to shop."

Noah had hopped out of the truck, and when he opened the back door, three giant bags spilled out onto the driveway.

Shocked, Shayna walked, hand in hand with Isabella, over to help Noah pick up the clothing that had fallen out of the bags.

"Lord, Noah." Shayna picked up two of the bags to carry them into the house. "What in the world did you buy?"

"It feels like I bought out the entire blasted store," he grumbled. "Women can be vicious during a back-to-school sale."

"Told you." Isabella sighed dramatically.

"Shopping during a major sale can be a bit of a blood sport." She laughed. "Don't worry, you guys. Come on in and we'll get it all sorted out."

Noah gave her a quick peck on the cheek when he walked through the open front door of her house. He unceremoniously dropped the bags of clothing on the couch.

"Is it okay if I hunt for some food in your fridge?" he asked. "It was so crazy that the lines for food were twenty and thirty people deep."

"Forage away," she said.

Isabella ignored the bags of clothing and went over to love on Pilot.

"Hey, Isabella," Shayna said. "Do you want to see what arrived today?"

The girl hugged Pilot and reassured him that she would be right back before she bounced up and trotted over to Shayna. They both walked into the formal living room. Stacked neatly in the corner were packages with Fragile written on the boxes.

Isabella spotted them immediately, ran over to the packages and slid part of the way on her knees.

"Are these the new ornaments?"

Shayna clasped her hands excitedly. "Or-na-ments!"

Shayna had asked Isabella to help her pick out ornaments; Shayna loved ornaments that were miniatures of real items and anything that was interactive, like a tiny snow globe or a music box that played a tune when wound. Isabella had been particularly attracted to Disney ornaments and everything Santa Claus.

"Can we open them now?"

"I've been waiting for you." Shayna lifted the packages and brought them over to the coffee table.

Together, they opened the boxes and unwrapped each ornament. Most were in collector's boxes and easily stacked. Whenever Shayna acquired a new ornament, it felt like a small part of her childhood pain around Christmas was replaced by the joy.

Wanting Isabella to feel that same joy, Shayna opened the Disney princesses first. One after another, Isabella's princesses were lined up on the coffee table. The look of wonder on the girl's face gave Shayna such pleasure. It was so gratifying to share her love of Christmas with a child. She was way ahead of schedule with her decorations inside the house because of Isabella.

"Did you really need more ornaments?" Noah appeared, his brow furrowed. "You still have a ton in the garage out back."

"Are you okay?" She ignored his comment about the ornaments. "You look like you don't feel well."

"I have a headache," Noah told her.

"Let's go find you something for that." Shayna stood up, and they walked together into the kitchen.

Shayna got an over-the-counter painkiller and a glass of water. Noah took the pills and guzzled down the entire glass of water.

"Why don't you go lay down for a while? I'll go through the clothes with Isabella."

Noah stood up; the features of his handsome face were tight with fatigue, and his lovely sculpted lips were turned down.

"Are you sure?"

"One hundred percent."

"Thank you," Noah said gratefully. "Can I get a hug? I haven't even had a chance to properly greet you."

Shayna stepped into his embrace and hugged him; they both sighed when their bodies connected. It was undeniable that when they hugged they felt like a perfect fit.

"Go get some rest," she said. He gave her a quick kiss on the lips and then disappeared down the hallway.

Shayna and Isabella finished unpacking the new ornaments and then sat there together admiring their selections.

"We did good," she told the girl.

Isabella nodded with bright smile. "Can we put up a tree now so we can hang them?"

Even though she was an admitted Christmasaholic, she had never put up a tree *this* early. But, then again, she had never had Isabella in her life before.

"We can't decorate the tree that normally goes in here, because I always get a live tree."

Isabella's disappointment was written on her face.

"But," Shayna continued, "we *could* put up the tree that goes in the bay window by the front door."

Isabella's face was now aglow with anticipation. *"Today?"*

Shayna laughed happily. "Not today. But soon."

Noah fell asleep the minute his head hit the pillow, and when he woke up, his headache was gone. He went to the bathroom to splash water on his face before going to find Shayna and his daughter.

"How's it going in here?"

Shayna was folding one of the shirts he had purchased, and Isabella was playing on Shayna's tablet with her head resting on the corner of Pilot's fluffy bed.

"We went through all of the clothing." Shayna put her hand on a small stack of clothes and a sparkly unicorn backpack. "This is what we can keep."

Noah slumped onto the couch. "Say what now?"

Shayna pointed to the overstuffed bags. "All of those need to be returned."

"No." Noah voiced his gut reaction. "I'm not going back there."

"Most of those clothes aren't even her size, Noah. Didn't you have her try anything on?"

"Heck no," Noah said. "We couldn't even get near the dressing rooms. I'm telling you, it was brutal."

"Well, she can't go to school with four shirts, a pair of jeans, one pair of socks and a backpack."

"I'm not taking any of that back," he reiterated. "I'll donate it."

Shayna sat down next to him on the couch. "Next time, I'll go with you."

"How about if I just give you my credit card and the two of you go?"

"And have you miss all of the fun?" she said teasingly. "Not a chance."

They made an entire day of it. First, they went back to the stores to exchange, return, and buy clothes for Isabella. Shayna had no idea how much fun it could be to pick out outfits for a little girl; she had loved every second of that experience. And it helped that Isabella was as cute a button and looked good in anything she tried on. The two of them had discovered yet another thing they had in common: shopping for all things with sequins! They shopped while Noah waited in a nearby chair; when they had made all of their selections, Noah paid. It was the perfect working relationship.

After shopping, they stopped off at a diner to eat. After lunch, and as promised, the three of them set up one of her Christmas trees.

"This is a monster." Noah climbed up on the ladder and snapped the top part of the massive tree into place.

The tree, one of Shayna's favorites, was chock-full of multicolored optical lights that flashed and twinkled in a way that always delighted her. Shayna showed Isabella how to fluff up the branches and fill in any bare spots that detracted from the illusion that the tree was a real fir. One by one, they placed Isabella's princesses on the tree. They were given the best real estate. Next, they hung up the Santa Clauses. Isabella had picked out a Santa Claus on an exercise bike that, when wound, made Santa pedal the bike in the most charming way. Another Santa Claus was kissing Mrs. Claus under the mistletoe.

"Now all we need are some candy canes for the tree." Shayna stepped back to critique their work.

"And a star." Isabella stepped back to stand by her, lending her critical eye.

"You're right," Shayna agreed. "Would you like to pick out the star for this tree?"

"Uh-huh!" Isabella gave a huge, definitive nod.

"You're spoiling her," Noah said after Isabella took Pilot out to the backyard.

"She deserves it."

Noah tugged her into his arms and hugged her tightly. He looked down into her face. "Have I told you lately that I love you?"

Shayna smiled up at him. "Not for at least the last hour."

He kissed her gently on the lips. "I love you, Dr. Wade."

"I love you, Captain Brand."

Together they walked to the back door, wanting to enjoy the last remnants of summer. Soon, it would be fall, and they would have to start bringing out their cold-weather clothing.

"You have a special way with her," Noah said. "I couldn't imagine doing this without you."

"Well," Shayna told him, "I do have an advantage. I *was* a little girl."

Isabella insisted on staying until it was dark enough to really see the lights on the Christmas tree. After dinner, and after lighting the Christmas tree, Isabella had wandered upstairs to her old room in the finished attic and promptly fell asleep.

"You can stay," Shayna told Noah. "There's no sense waking her up."

"Are you sure?"

"Of course."

The night was cool, and there was a full moon in the sky. Shayna grabbed a bottle of wine and glasses while Noah carried a blanket out to the backyard. Lately, and after many make-out sessions, Shayna was beginning to feel ready to take the next step physically with Noah. Her body was craving his touch, and, although the kissing and cuddling was wonderful, it was becoming more of a source of frustration. Her body wanted to be satisfied even when her brain was stomping on the brakes.

Noah unfolded the blanket and laid it on the grass. Shayna joined him on the blanket and held the glasses while he poured them some wine. They touched glasses, and Noah said, as he always did, "Here's to us."

Two glasses of wine down the hatch, Shayna put

her glass aside so she could lie down next to Noah. The wine had served to relax her while all her senses seemed to heighten. The smell of his skin mixed with the sweet night air and lavender from her flowers was an aphrodisiac.

"Hmm." She buried her nose into his neck. "You smell so good."

"So do you." Noah turned his body toward her so he could kiss her in the moonlight.

Noah hadn't tried to even get to second base with her; perhaps he was as worried about crossing that line as she was. But her body wanted what it wanted. Shayna captured his hand and placed it on her breast. Her breast filled his large, strong hand, and she felt the warmth of his skin through the thin material of her blouse.

Noah massaged her breast, playing with the nipple, and the friction of the lace of her bra made her nipple hard and taut. He kissed her deeply, and she tasted the sweetness of the wine on his tongue.

Emboldened, Noah slipped his hand beneath her blouse and pushed her bra aside.

"Oh," Shayna gasped and pushed her breast into his hand.

Noah broke their kiss to ask, "Do you want more?"

"Yes," she gasped. She did want more of him. More kissing, more touching, more pleasure.

"Finally," Noah growled and kissed her with renewed passion.

When Shayna gave him the green light to deepen their physical connection, he was beyond ready. He had wanted to take it slow, but Shayna was moving at a pace that would make a turtle frustrated.

Noah unbuttoned her blouse and pushed her bra aside so he could feast on her beautiful, large, natural breast. His lips found her nipple to suckle. Shayna held on to the back of his head, making the most satisfying gasps of pleasure. The weight of her breast in his hand and the taste of her skin made his body stand at attention. And he could tell by the way she was breathing and seeking out his body that her need to be joined with him, to be given a release, was just as strong. It was the first time he had truly *felt* that Shayna desired him in the same way he had been desiring her.

He knew he had to wait. He knew that he needed to have more self-control. But she didn't have to suffer. Noah knew that he could give her what she needed, and he wanted, more than anything, to send her up into the clouds with his lips and his hands.

Noah was just about to unbutton her pants when Pilot, still inside the house, began to bark.

The spell broken, Shayna sat up. "Pilot only barks if someone rings the doorbell."

Noah groaned in frustration. "Who could be coming over at this hour?"

Shayna quickly buttoned up her blouse. "I don't know."

Together, they gathered up the glasses, the bottle and the blanket. Noah followed her in, feeling irritated that their intimate moment had been interrupted.

Shayna looked through the peephole, and he heard her say, "It can't be."

"Who is it?" Noah joined her at the door.

"It's Annika," she said in a whisper. "Annika is here."

Chapter Fourteen

Noah had been punched in the gut a time or two in his life. Shayna saying that Annika was on the other side of the door felt exactly like a full-grown man balling up his fist and pile driving a punch into his stomach. A wave of anxiety, anger and shock rocked his core, and he actually felt a bit nauseous at the thought of seeing his ex again.

"Play nice." Shayna's voice, ever calm and steady, served to anchor him to the present moment.

Shayna opened the door, and he was, for the first time in nearly a decade, standing in front of Annika. What he had imagined didn't match reality. The woman who stood before him now barely resembled the fresh, perky, sassy picture he had held in his mind. The Annika of today was slim—almost painfully so—and her shoulders were slumped forward, making her seem even more petite than her five-one frame. The features of her face seemed tight and pinched; her wispy hair, a bit greasy and darker than before, was pulled back into a ponytail. Even her eyes, the same sable color he remembered, appeared dull and sad.

"Hi, Shayna." Annika's voice was raspy. "Hi, Noah."

"I left messages for you at the rehab facility." Noah didn't feel like being polite or cordial. Why did Annika deserve that, after all she had put everyone through?

Annika stood with her arms twisted in front of her body. "I got them."

He tried not to raise his voice but failed. "But you didn't bother to respond."

Shayna touched his arm. "You don't want to wake Isabella."

Annika's eyes widened and became watery at the sound of her daughter's name, and he was afraid she was going to start crying. He didn't want to feel sympathy for her; if she cried, he just might.

"Mom thought she might still be here," Annika said.

Noah had sent a video to May of him tucking Isabella into the bed upstairs.

"When did you talk to May?" he asked, and he did hear the accusation in his tone. If May had known that Annika was coming to town, she should have let him know. But, of course, once again, the minute Annika appeared on the scene, the tenuous trust he had built with Isabella's grandmother crumbled into dust.

Instead of answering him directly, Annika said, "I've come home to take care of Mom."

Noah waited, his eyes drilling down on every expression that appeared on Annika's face.

His ex continued, "I'm here to pick up Isabella and take her back to Mom's house."

Noah used his body—his wide shoulders and his military stance—to block the doorway. "Think again, Annika."

Shayna stepped up to stand beside him. "Why don't the two of you go out to the gazebo and talk? You don't want to wake Isabella."

Noah clenched his teeth to stop himself from verbally unloading the rage he had felt ever since he had first found out about Isabella.

"Come in, Annika." Shayna used her arm to move him back a bit and opened the door to her house to welcome Annika into her world. Part of him resented the fact that she wasn't emoting the same anger toward his ex as he felt, but part of him was grateful that Shayna was taking the neutral position.

"Thank you," Annika said quietly to Shayna.

Once inside, his ex's eyes bounced from one place to another to absorb the lovely features of the home Shayna had made for herself.

"You have such a beautiful home, Shayna," his ex said.

"Thank you." Shayna closed the door gently. "I'm proud of it."

"It's already Christmas in here," Annika said. "I remember how much you always loved Christmas. You know, I actually took Isabella to see your Christmas display when she was one or two years old. She laughed the entire time."

Noah wanted to throw a verbal dart at everything Annika said; he wanted to remind her of every moment he had missed with his daughter because of her lies. If Shayna hadn't been there—if Isabella wasn't upstairs sleeping—he doubted that this first meeting would be as polite as it had been so far.

"I'm glad." Shayna led them back to the French doors that opened into her backyard. "I want everyone to feel the magic and joy of Christmas when they see my display."

Noah noticed that Annika was gravitating toward Shayna, addressing her, looking at her, while she had barely looked at him once or twice.

Before she went outside, Annika said to Shayna, "Mom told me that you let Isabella pick out the theme for this year."

"Yes, I did," Shayna said in a kind voice. "She wanted the theme to be princesses—not exactly a typical Christmas theme, but we're making it work."

Annika reached for Shayna's hand and squeezed it. "Thank you."

"You're welcome, Annika." His best friend's willingness to be so warm and fuzzy with his ex made him angry with Shayna. She was supposed to be on *his* side. "She's a great kid."

Noah met Shayna's eyes, and he knew she was silently telling him "play nice" as he followed Annika out the door and into the backyard. They walked with several feet between them; he didn't want to be physically near her, and he sensed that she felt the same way about him. It struck Noah as rotten luck or bad karma when they walked over the very grass where he had been kissing Shayna.

"After you." He gestured with his hand for Annika to enter the gazebo first.

Once seated, they both seemed at a loss for words. It was strange and awkward and downright unpleasant to be with Annika again. Particularly when he hadn't been able to prepare for it mentally.

"Shayna has really made something of herself, hasn't she?" Annika asked.

"She's an amazing woman."

"I felt like I was interrupting something…"

"We're together." Noah's tone was razor-sharp.

"I always thought that would happen."

There was a long lull in the conversation before she said, "I know you've had a DNA test done on my daughter."

"I have established paternity," he said bluntly. "And I think the phrase you're looking for is *our* daughter."

In a nearly inaudible whisper, Annika repeated, "Our daughter."

"I didn't know for sure she was yours." She added, "I wasn't sure, so I just thought of her as mine."

"You put Millburn on the birth certificate. You had her call him *Daddy*. That was my privilege, not his."

She didn't defend her actions, and he was glad that she didn't try.

"When I found out I was pregnant, I quit everything," she said after another lull. "And she was perfect. A perfect little girl."

Noah's brother Shane had struggled with drugs and alcohol after he left the military. Shane still had support from the VA and attended meetings regularly. So, through his brother's experience, he did have—at least intellectually—an understanding of the nature of Annika's addiction. He knew it was an illness—and he also knew that relapse was a real possibility.

"You're not taking her tonight, Annika," Noah said, his voice firm. If he had been hoping for some apology from his ex, he would have been disappointed. She didn't apologize, and he doubted very much that she would *ever* acknowledge the pain and damage her lies had caused.

"Mom has custody." It was the strongest he had heard her voice sound.

"For now," he countered. "May can't take care of herself, much less Isabella. And you've just gotten out of rehab."

"I'm here to help Mom. She's supposed to get discharged early next week." Annika crossed her arms tightly, protectively, in front of her slender body. "I already have a sponsor here, and I'm going to attend my first meeting tomorrow."

"Good," he said. "I'm glad."

And he was glad—for Isabella's sake, he was sincerely glad.

"Are you going to try to take her overseas?" Annika's voice was laced with genuine fear.

"That's not my immediate plan, no." Actually, that thought hadn't crossed his mind.

Annika suddenly stood up; she wiped her palms on her jeans before she said, "I should go."

It was an abrupt end, but Noah was glad for it.

"I'm coming back in the morning. I need to see Isabella."

They walked in silence back to the house. Once inside, Shayna walked Annika to the door and, of course, told Annika that she should plan on joining them for breakfast.

"How did it go?" Shayna asked him once Annika was gone.

"Just hug me." Noah opened his arms for her.

Shayna stepped into his arms, and they held each other tightly for many minutes. Noah rested his chin lightly on the top of Shayna's head, grateful for the comfort her embrace always afforded him.

"That was a shock to the system," he said.

"Yes, it was."

"How are you?" he asked, knowing that beneath Shayna's calm demeanor there had to be a Pandora's box of emotions.

"Tired," she said with a sigh.

"Should I sleep in the guest room?" he asked, hoping that she would want him close to her as he wanted to be close to her.

Shayna stepped out of his arms, took his hand and led him to her bedroom. They both climbed into her king-size bed and snuggled close to each other. It seemed to Noah that Shayna needed what he needed: comfort and safety. Annika was a stick of dynamite that, if lighted, could rock the fragile foundation they had built over the last few weeks.

"I love you, Shayna," Noah said, his nose buried in her silky-soft, sweet-smelling hair.

Shayna shut off the light and then snuggled more deeply into the bed; she threaded her fingers with his and moved his arm more tightly into her body.

"I love you, Noah," she said sleepily. "Everything is going to be okay."

Noah didn't sleep much that night, and he didn't try to make love to Shayna. He didn't want the first time they were intimate to be marred by Annika's reappearance in their lives. He had spooned Shayna most of the night, and, somewhere along the way, Pilot had climbed into the bed. When he awakened the next morning, feeling groggy, Shayna was gone and Pilot was spooning him.

He smelled breakfast cooking; he got out of bed, took a quick shower and then joined his favorite girls in the kitchen.

"Good morning." Noah gave Shayna a quick kiss.

"Good morning."

Isabella was watching a YouTube video.

"What are you watching?" He sat down on the stool next to her.

"This kid playing Minecraft," Isabella said, not looking up from the screen.

Noah exchanged looks with Shayna. "That's a thing?"

"Apparently so." She scraped the scrambled eggs onto a plate and then covered them with a paper towel. "How are you doing?"

"I've got to adapt and overcome," he said. Noah had spent a lot of time thinking about his interaction with Annika the night before. It was difficult for him to connect with the person who had once idolized her. The one thing that he needed to guard against was letting his anger be on display; he needed to find a way to play it cool, no matter how many buttons she pushed. And the truth was, Annika knew where every single one of his buttons was hidden.

A soft knock on the door made Noah's gut twist into that uncomfortable knot again. Shayna dried her hands on a towel. "Do me a favor, Isabella. Go see who's at the door."

Isabella watched the video a second or two longer before she put down her tablet and skipped over to the door. She opened the door and let out a surprised scream that made Pilot woof.

"Mommy!" Isabella threw herself into Annika's arms.

Annika had knelt down and absorbed her daughter.

"Bella baby." Annika had tears streaming down her face.

"Mommy." Isabella was crying, too.

"I've missed you so much." Annika said, wiping her daughter's tears off her face.

"Where have you been?" There were fresh tears on Isabella's face.

"I was sick," his ex said. "I needed to go to a place where I could get better."

"You were sick?"

Annika hugged her daughter again as she nodded her head. "I was, baby, but Mama's better now."

Isabella played with her mother's wispy, freshly washed hair that was pulled back into a simple ponytail. "Can we go home?"

That knot in Noah's gut twisted tighter when his daughter asked to go home. He wanted Isabella to know that *he* was her home, too.

Annika looked over their daughter's head to meet his gaze; she ran her fingers through Isabella's thick, dark locks. "We'll see, baby."

Shayna had filled the table with comfort food—biscuits, eggs, bacon, grits and homemade waffles. She had already had her cheat day, but she piled her plate high and then went back for seconds. That was the only way he knew that she was not as comfortable with Annika at her table, in her house, as she was projecting on the outside.

Isabella was the one who kept the conversation

going. She wanted to tell her mom everything, from riding horses at Sugar Creek to learning how to paint. His daughter barely ate any of her food because she was so busy talking. And, he noticed, she kept touching Annika's arm, as if she were worried that her mother was going to disappear into thin air. Noah hadn't said more than a couple of words to Annika—in truth, he just didn't have anything nice to say to her, and the last thing he wanted to do was be combative with her in front of Isabella. Shayna, as she always did, filled in the gaps in conversation for the both of them.

"Thank you, so much." Annika helped clear the table when breakfast was done.

"You're welcome." Shayna put the dishes in the sink. "I was happy to do it."

"Well, pretty girl." Annika looked down into her daughter's upturned face. "I'd better get going."

"Where are you going?" Isabella's voice went up two octaves. She clung to Annika's arm and began to cry. "Take me with you!"

Noah saw the crestfallen look on Annika's face. "I'm going to see Nanna. But I'll come back to see you. I promise."

"I want to go with you!" his daughter wailed. He'd never heard or seen her like this, and it was heartbreaking.

"Noah." Shayna touched his shoulder.

He was in an impossible position—could he trust Annika with Isabella? Was she really sober? How could he explain to Isabella that she couldn't go with her mother when all he was to her, at least for now, was a fun friend of the family?

"Hey." Annika held her daughter's face in her hands. "It's going to be okay. You'll see."

"I think May would love to see you," Noah said.

Annika's dark brown eyes widened when she realized that he was agreeing to let Isabella go with her. She mouthed the words *thank you*, and he gave her a slight nod in return.

After Isabella put on her tennis shoes that lit up with every step she took, mother and daughter walked hand in hand to the door. Noah followed them and then watched from the doorway as Annika took the car seat from his truck and put it into her faded, dinged-up Hyundai. When they pulled out of the driveway, Isabella waved at him from the back seat.

"You made the right decision." Shayna met him at the door and hugged him.

"I think I made the only decision I could make," he said. "I don't have custody, and she's Isabella's mother."

"I thought of that, too."

"She seemed *okay*, right?"

"A little bit fragile and shaky, but if either one of us believed she wasn't sober, we wouldn't have let her take Isabella."

He nodded his agreement; then he sensed Shayna studying him, and he looked her way.

"How does it feel?" she asked, her eyes intent on his face.

"How does what feel?"

"To see her again?"

"Annika?" He said her name with a large dose of disgust. "I could've gone the rest of my life without seeing her again."

The weeks after Annika's arrival back into his life were a mixed bag of emotions. He had been temporarily relieved of the burden of being an instant father. Annika appeared to be on a good path; in fact, his brother Shane had mentioned seeing her at meetings, and Isabella was over the moon to be living with her mother and May again. Noah was determined to assert himself as Isabella's father, but, after a couple of sessions with Dr. Friend, he understood that it was going to be a marathon, not a sprint. His daughter was going to need some time to adjust to a new normal and a second father. May, Annika and he had an appointment with a mediator the following week, and he was confident that they could iron out the details of their situation, starting with how and when Isabella would be told that he was her father. He did miss having Isabella at the ranch with his family; she was a bundle of bright light and happy energy. But he knew that the details of custody and visitation would unfold with time. And in all honesty, he hadn't figured out how to continue with his life as a marine without missing more of Isabella's growing-up years.

The area of his life that didn't seem to be moving in the right direction was his relationship with Shayna. Ever since Annika had returned, he felt that Shayna had erected a giant wall between them. And Annika seemed to be everywhere, all the time! If Isabella was at Shayna's house to work on the Christmas installation, Annika was invited, too. Noah knew that he had to make peace with Annika, but the whiplash—going from finding out that she had kept a child hidden from him to having her hanging out with Shayna all the time—was more than Noah could handle gracefully.

"What the heck?" Noah pulled up to Shayna's house, which was overflowing with people. He parked his truck on the road outside Shayna's house, because there were too many vehicles already parked in her driveway. When he stepped out of his truck, he heard Christmas music blaring and saw that many of the college kids in the front yard were wearing Santa hats. He'd thought he was coming over to spend some much-needed alone time with Shayna. Instead, he had found a party.

Noah walked up the driveway, searching for Shayna. When he found her, he wasn't at all happy with what he saw.

"Noah!" Shayna spotted him and waved her paintbrush in the air. "The princesses have arrived!"

Sitting next to Shayna, also holding a paintbrush was, of course, Annika. Isabella came barreling out of the front door; when she saw him, she ran over to him, gave him a quick hug and then shouted, "Noah! The princesses are here!"

"I see this," he said, disappointed that he wouldn't have alone time with Shayna.

When Shayna heard Isabella call out his name, she turned her head and saw him standing nearby. With a big smile on her face, she stood up, brushed the grass off her jeans and trotted over to him with a big smile on her pretty face. Her hair was piled up on top of her head, there were flecks of paint on her face and on her hands, and she was glowing with excitement. She hugged him and then turned to survey the work that was happening on the front lawn.

"Can you believe it? All of the princesses arrived today." She slipped her glasses up onto the top of her head.

"I thought we were going to have dinner."

He watched her closely and saw a flash of sheepishness race across her features. "I know. I'm sorry. When the guys told me that the princesses were done, I just couldn't wait to get them on site and start painting."

"I understand." And he did understand—to a point. He put his arm around her shoulders; it really bothered him to feel how her body stiffened when he touched her. "I would like a minute alone with you."

"Is everything okay?" she asked, her brow wrinkled with concern.

"Let's talk inside."

The only place they could truly have privacy with all the volunteers wandering in and out of the house was her bedroom.

"What's wrong?" Shayna sat down on the corner of the bed.

"Why is Annika here?" Noah cut right to his main issue. "It seems like every time I come over, she's here."

Genuine surprise flashed in Shayna's forest green eyes and he almost, *almost* regretted asking the question.

"Isabella wanted to come over to paint the princesses. She asked if her mom could come. What was I supposed to say?"

Noah ran his hands over his head several times. "Are the two of you becoming friends or something?"

"I don't know." Shayna asked defensively, "Why shouldn't we?"

"You do realize that I'm not looking for a sister-wife situation, right?"

"Noah...come on."

"I'm serious," Noah said. "I don't want to see Annika all of the time."

"You have a child with her. You're going to see her."

"I don't need reminding of that, Shay. I need to figure out how to coparent with her, and I will. But that doesn't mean that we need to socialize with her, does it?"

Shayna frowned at him. "I don't understand why you're getting so upset. She's had a rough time—she's really fragile, and she needs as many people to support her as possible. She needs to feel accepted and safe. I know what it's like to be the child of a parent who struggles with substance abuse."

"I know you do..."

"If I can do anything to stop Isabella from going through what I went through, I'm going to do it," Shayna added in a pointed manner. "And, frankly, I don't need your permission to invite anyone I damn well please to my house."

Noah breathed in deeply and blew it out quickly. He stared at Shayna hard; he knew her too well. Yes, of course she wanted to help Annika. That was her nature—always fighting for the underdog. But there was more to this than Shayna was willing to admit.

"Look, the bottom line is that ever since Annika came back, you've been pushing me away."

Shayna shook her head.

"Yes, you have." He refused to be thrown off the scent.

"I've been busy." She averted her eyes, and that was when he knew he was right.

"You've been pushing me away and shoving me in Annika's direction," Noah said. "I feel like you've actually been trying to set me up with her on mini dates. Asking us to run to the store together, putting us together on a project... Tell me I'm wrong, Shay."

Shayna bit her lip, and it took her what seemed like a very long time to respond. "If there is even the tiniest chance that you and Annika can get back together..."

Noah took a step toward her. "That's not going to happen."

"If Isabella could have both of her parents living under the same roof..."

Noah took her hands in his, coaxed her to stand up so he could look into her eyes and let her look into his. He wanted her to see the truth of his words reflected in his eyes. "Shayna. Please listen to me. That's *never* going to happen."

Shayna looked into his eyes, and it felt like the first

time in a while that she wasn't shutting him out. "How do you know if you don't try, Noah? Annika is back—she's not with Jasper...you have a daughter with her."

"It's not going to happen because I don't love her." Noah held her face gently in his hands. "I love you."

Shayna had unshed tears swimming in her eyes. It broke his heart when he saw how genuinely upset she was. "I don't want to get in the way of Isabella having her parents together...if there's even the slimmest chance..."

"You're not getting in the way." He worked to reassure her with the directness and honesty in his eyes. "That's not an option for Annika or me."

"Are you sure?" she asked, her eyes so intent on his face.

"I've never been more sure of anything in my life, Shay." He kissed her lips. "I was a kid when I was with Annika, Shay. I'm a man now. And this man wants to spend the rest of his life with you."

Chapter Fifteen

Shayna pulled up to the main house at Sugar Creek Ranch and realized that this was the first Sunday morning breakfast that she was going to attend as Noah's *girlfriend*. She had never been nervous around Noah's family—in many ways, they felt like family already—but today, walking up to the grand entryway to the house, she felt an odd mix of excitement and anxiety.

"Shayna!" Lilly answered the door with a welcome smile. "We are so happy that you could join us."

"Thank you, Lilly." Shayna hugged Noah's mother—Lilly always had a way of making her feel welcome and calm.

"Noah should be on the back patio." Lilly linked her arm with hers and led her through the foyer, into a enormous great room with vaulted ceilings and rough-hewn wood beams that had been harvested from Sugar Creek land.

"I'm glad that my son finally found the diamond among all of the lumps of coal he usually fishes out of the barrel."

Shayna felt her cheeks flush with pleasure. She understood Lilly perfectly—it was her way of giving the relationship a stamp of approval. Lilly escorted her all the way to the French doors leading out to the patio. The moment Noah saw her, he left his conversation with his brothers Colt and Shane, and he strode over to greet her.

"You look amazing." He took her hand in his and kissed her on the lips right in front of his family.

"So do you." It still felt surreal that Noah was *hers*. She had dreamed it, she had tried to manifest it, but when it finally happened, it was difficult to accept.

The entire family greeted Shayna with the same acceptance that Lilly had shown. And after she had made the rounds, it struck her that her worries about transitioning from best friend to love interest with Noah's family were completely unfounded. It seemed, in retrospect, silly.

Noah tucked her hand into the crook of his arm and then placed his hand over hers as they strolled the manicured grounds surrounding the main house.

"Isabella should arrive soon," Noah told her.

Noah had seemed much more relaxed ever since he had gotten through mediation with Annika and May. For now, May would retain full custody, Annika had agreed to regular drug tests and updates from her sponsor, the birth certificate would be updated to reflect Noah as the biological father, and Noah was granted liberal visitation rights. Dr. Friend had facilitated the conversation between Annika and Isabella, and his daughter had taken it, for the most part, in stride.

"I don't really know if she will ever feel comfortable calling me Dad." They had paused near a fence overlooking a pasture where a herd of horses was grazing in the distance.

"It's going to take time." Shayna leaned into his body, feeling more comfortable day by day with the change in the physical aspect of her relationship with Noah.

He had his arm around her shoulders; he kissed the top of her head—a familiar gesture of affection that they had always shared. They both enjoyed the silence while they admired the landscape.

"Noah!" his brother Shane hollered from the patio. "Annika is here!"

"We're coming." Noah waved his hand to let Shane know that he had heard him.

Before they headed back to the house, Noah dipped his head down and caught her eye. "Promise me you won't ask her in for breakfast."

Shayna gave him a self-effacing smile. "I promise. No more trying to set you up with your ex-fiancée."

"Hallelujah!" Noah tilted his head back with a hearty laugh she hadn't heard since he had returned to Bozeman.

Hand in hand, they walked quickly back to the house,

both excited to spend time with Isabella and his family. Shayna felt for the first time like she belonged with Noah—not just as his ride-or-die friend, but as his lover, his companion and his safe harbor in a storm. And as they ascended the steps to the patio, surrounded by the loud, boisterous voices of his family, Shayna realized that they were walking into their future—and she knew, without question, that she was in the right place, with the right man, at exactly the right time for their story to begin.

As promised, Shayna *did not* invite Annika to Sunday breakfast, but she did give her a hug when they greeted her at the door. For Shayna, it wasn't always easy to have Annika around—it often dredged up memories from her adolescence that she would prefer to keep buried—but she knew that the focus had to be on Isabella.

"Hi, Princess Isabella." Shayna gave the girl a hug.

"Hi." Isabella scrunched up her face playfully and handed her a piece of paper.

"What's this?" Shayna unfolded it and shared it with Noah.

"It's a family tree," Noah's daughter said, spinning around in a circle.

Annika bent down, caught her daughter up in her arms, hugged her and then kissed her on the cheek. "They made family trees in school this week."

"Isabella," Noah said, "this is beautiful."

Isabella laughed when her mom kissed her several

times on the cheek before she broke away to peek over the edge of the paper.

"That's Dad Number One and Mom," she explained. "That's Nanna."

Noah pointed to two additional stick people on the tree.

"That's you, Dad Number Two," Isabella said very seriously. "And this is Shayna with Pilot."

"Is this for me?" Noah asked his daughter.

She nodded her head and then asked, "Can I go see the horses?"

"After breakfast," Noah promised her. To Annika, he said, "We'll drop her off by five."

Shayna was proud of Noah—he had a ways to go with Annika, but his face didn't turn red and his jaw didn't clench the minute he saw the mother of his child. He was still stiff and brief yet relatively cordial.

Isabella raced into the house and went straight to the kitchen, where she knew that she would find Lilly. Grandmother and granddaughter—without those labels—had created a strong bond while Isabella had been living at the ranch.

"Annika looks so much better, doesn't she?" Shayna asked him in a private voice.

Noah was still looking at the family tree Isabella had given to him. "What? I don't know. I guess."

"She's put on weight, and her color's better. I actually suggested that she go see Blake. She wants to get back into shape and teach gymnastics," Shayna told a disinterested Noah.

Instead of answering her, Noah showed her the picture again. "We actually made it onto the tree."

"Yes, Noah." Shayna held on to his arm and laughed at his amazement. "We certainly did."

"I'm stuffed!" Shayna happily complained. "I can't believe that your family eats like this every Sunday."

Noah smiled at her from behind the wheel of his truck. "You've got to pace yourself, that's for sure."

While Lilly took Isabella for a horseback ride, Noah had said that he wanted to "steal her away" for some alone time. Knowing that she loved to hike, Noah was taking some back roads through the ranch to pick up a hiking trail that would lead them to a lookout that was a family favorite.

"I'm so ready to walk off all of that food." Shayna climbed out of the truck and shut the door. Lately, Noah had stopped resisting her lifestyle change and had begun to support it.

Together, they walked up a trail, stopping occasionally to allow her to catch her breath. "You know that I wouldn't have been able to make it up to the peak last year."

"I'm really impressed with how much you can do now," he said, offering her his hand while she found a foothold in a rocky crevice.

"It's like I'm living a whole new life!"

They reached the peak, enjoying the feel of the late-morning sun on their skin. Noah found a smooth area of the large sheets of rock that covered the peak for them to rest.

"Look at this view," Shayna marveled. "I've never been up here before."

Noah handed her a bottle of water he had carried in a backpack for them. "I've wanted to share this with you for a long time."

She guzzled the water and then twisted the cap back on. "And now you can."

He put his arm around her shoulders. Sitting at the top of the mountain with Noah at her side, overlooking the expansive land holdings of his family, Shayna felt triumphant—lucky, blessed and triumphant.

"You know, Lee cornered me in the kitchen before you arrived and asked me what my intentions are with you."

Surprised, Shayna shifted her attention from the view to his handsome profile.

"I'm sorry," she said. "I didn't tell her to do that."

"I know," he said. "I didn't think you did."

Lee had always been a protector, and she was, understandably, skeptical of Noah's motives. But ultimately, it didn't matter to her what other people thought—it only mattered how Noah made her feel.

Noah met her gaze and held it. "Do you want to know what I told her?"

The way he was looking at her—like a man who was admiring the woman he loved—Shayna still felt butterflies in her stomach.

"Okay."

"I told her that my intention was to marry you."

Noah smiled mischievously at the fact that he had stunned her into silence. And then he kissed her. So sweetly and lovingly that all she could focus on was the clean scent of his skin and the strength of his hands as they held her close.

"I want to marry you, Shayna," Noah said between kisses.

She put her hand on his face, caught up in the blue ocean of his eyes.

"I want to have a family with you," he whispered against her lips.

"This is a dream," Shayna said softly.

"Then don't wake up, my love." Noah dropped butterfly kisses on her cheeks and her neck, the wonderful feel of his lips and his breath sending shivers of sheer pleasure dancing across her skin. "Never wake up."

After their romantic hike to the mountain peak, Shayna said goodbye to the family and headed back to her house. Noah had promised to stop by after he dropped off Isabella, and she wanted to make sure that she got some research done before he arrived. One of the hardest parts of being in a new relationship with Noah was her desire to ignore her work and spend all her free time with him. Especially when she knew that he was going to be heading back overseas in the distant future. They hadn't even begun to really discuss how their long-distance relationship would work—neither of them seemed ready to face that inevitable reality. It was much more fun to focus on the magic of the romance they were enjoying. Reality would inevitably smack them in the face soon enough.

After getting in a couple hours of research for her book, Shayna went to the detached garage to examine the paint on the bigger-than-life princesses. She was ahead of schedule on the installation, which allowed her to give herself the luxury of spending more time with Noah before he returned to Japan. Once she had inspected the wooden princesses and made some mental notes on how to improve their overall appearance, Shayna headed back to the house to get ready for her evening in with Noah. She took a shower, washed her hair, shaved her legs and then, after she dried off, she slathered lotion all over her body so her skin would feel silky soft to the touch. She shrugged into her robe before she sat down at her vanity and dried her hair.

In her bedroom, she opened her underwear drawer and found a sexy lace bra and panty set that she had purchased once she had begun to see results from working out with Blake. Shayna dropped the robe and looked at herself in the full-length mirror. The lacy black bra made her large breasts look perky and round and, to her eye, tantalizing. The panties followed the curve of her hourglass hips. She had never in her life worn lingerie for a man; Shayna was glad that Noah would be the first.

Shayna slipped into slim-fit jeans and a T-shirt. She leaned down to kiss Pilot on the head. "I think you're going to have to sleep in the living room tonight, my handsome fellow."

"Shayna?" Noah had used his key, which she had given to him earlier in the week.

Shayna came out from the bedroom, hoping that her effort would pay off. Barefoot, she met him at the door.

"For me?" he said, his eyes skimming across her body.

Shayna twirled around in a small circle flirtatiously. Before she could make a full rotation, Noah scooped her up into his strong arms and carried her to the bedroom. Pilot tried to follow behind him, but Noah used the heel of his boot to close the door before the dog could make it through the door.

"Sorry, old man," Noah said in a gravelly voice. "She's all mine tonight."

There had been an unspoken but palpable shift between them on the mountain. Noah had been patient and deferential while she became more comfortable with the physical side of their relationship. For her, it had been all about trust—trust in Noah's love for her, trust in his motives and trust in his ability to be faithful to her even when he was a world apart from her. Today on that mountain, Shayna knew, in her gut, that Noah was as dedicated to her as she was to him.

Noah's eyes had turned a deep, stormy blue as he laid her down on the bed. She loved how his eyes swept over her body, lingering on her breasts and the apex of her thighs. She wanted him. And he wanted her.

"Are you sure?" he asked her.

She nodded her head silently. Her body had ached for him for so long; all she could think of now was joining her body with his.

Noah stripped off his shirt; he was lean from years of running and had a six-pack from his religious routine of sit-ups in the morning. Shayna had never been sexually forward, but the desire to touch Noah, to feel his muscles, changed that for her. She sat up, her legs curled up beneath her body, and ran her fingers over the ridges of his stomach and upward to his chest. Noah caught her hands as they explored his body, lifting her arms over her head so he could remove her shirt.

Noah made a satisfied growling sound in the back of his throat as his eyes fixed on her breasts hidden behind a flimsy piece of lace. Noah leaned her back into the bed, kissing her long and hard before he unbuttoned her jeans and slipped them down over her hips, down her legs and then discarded them in a pile with their shirts.

Shayna had thought ever since they had become more than friends that intimacy with Noah would be awkward or weird. Beyond building trust, this was one of the main reasons she hadn't jumped into bed with him, no matter how much she had wanted to. And she had held back because she knew that once they crossed that line, a platonic friendship was off the table should they fail. Shayna knew herself well enough to know that going back was not an option—good, bad or indifferent, they would only be able to move forward from here.

Noah stripped out of his jeans but left his boxer briefs on. Shayna had never felt so sexy or desired; she openly admired the outline of his hard shaft, and her body began to tingle and hum in all her most private places. Noah used the strength of his arms to hover his body above hers so he could kiss her nipples through the lace before he worked his way down, dropping sensual kisses along his journey to her lacy panties. Shayna held on to his biceps, loving the feel of his muscles tense and strong beneath her fingertips.

"May I?" Noah asked, his fingers toying with the waistband of her underwear. She knew what he was asking—what he was wanting.

"Yes," she said in a breathy voice.

Noah slowly, methodically, little by little, slipped her out of her underwear. She knew that he was drawing out the foreplay; he wanted her to be so ready for him that she would *need* to make love to him.

Then he was kneeling on the floor and gently coaxing her legs apart; Shayna gasped at the first touch of his tongue. She grabbed the comforter with both hands, closed her eyes and let him have his way with her.

"Noah!" She said his name between gasps of pleasure. "The top drawer."

Noah kissed his way back up her body; he put her arm behind her body, lifting her up so her back was arched. Noah easily unhooked her bra while he pressed his hard-on suggestively, teasingly, into her.

She wiggled beneath him, pushing against him, wanting to rip his underwear off, grab him and guide him inside her. Noah fondled her breasts; when he began to suck on her nipples, she couldn't hold back. She cried out his name, her head thrown back, as orgasmic shudders wracked her body.

Panting and feeling like she needed more of him, Shayna kissed his chest and reached down between them to capture him in her hand. She opened her eyes, her fingers wrapped around his stiff manhood. Noah's eyes were at half-mast, and there was an animalistic desire in his intense blue eyes.

"Did you come?" he asked her.

She nodded, not wanting to wait another minute to join their bodies.

His smile was seductive, and there was a growl in his voice. "Do you want another?"

"Quit teasing me, Noah!" she commanded. "Top drawer!"

While Noah fished a condom out from the drawer, kicked off his underwear and rolled the condom on, Shayna had moved into the middle of the bed, her head propped up on the pillows, her long, silky hair cascading over her beautiful breasts. Naked on the bed, her cheeks a pretty shade of pink and her chest rising and falling quickly from the pleasure he had already given her, Shayna resembled one of the voluptuous women in the Victorian-era paintings she loved so much.

Noah couldn't stop taking in her beauty—he was struck by it. She held out her arms for him, and he went to her. He covered her with his body and kissed her. The sounds she made when he had filled her body completely, bonding them together—heart, mind, body and soul.

Shayna wrapped her legs around his hips, taking him in and holding him tight. She was a perfect fit—so warm and slick. He found their rhythm and drove into her, so hard and so deep; he felt her coming before he heard it in her sweet moans.

"God, I love you, Shayna," Noah said over and over. The feel of her shuddering in his arms, the feel of her soft breasts pressed up against his chest, her scent, her taste—it all drove him wild. He thrust into her, harder, quicker, until he felt the dam break and he exploded.

Noah collapsed into her arms, giving her his weight for a split second while he caught his breath. He also needed to make sense of what just happened; it had never been like this before with any of the women he had known intimately. It was as if he had never actually made love before—until now—until Shayna.

He didn't want this incredible body-to-body connection to end; he reluctantly rolled onto his back beside her.

"That was incredible." Shayna had a lilting quality to her voice—she sounded happy and satisfied, and that was all because of him.

He laced his fingers with hers. "There's nothing better than making love to you, Shay."

He felt her turn her head toward him. "Worth the wait?"

"Abso-frickin'-lutely."

Shayna laughed and curled her body toward his. "Do you want to shower?"

"I thought you'd never ask," he said, ready for round two.

He hopped off the bed, discarded the condom in the trash can and held out his hand to her. "I've got a long list of things I've been wanting to do to you in the shower."

"Wait a minute." Shayna gave him a perplexed look, and her cute expression made him grin. "You want me to shower with you?"

"You bet." Noah extended his hand again. "I'm going to lather you up, rinse you off and then lick the water off every inch of that sexy body of yours. How does that sound?"

Shayna didn't take much time to come to her decision. She placed her hand into his and said, "Yes, please."

Shayna stepped out of the steaming-hot shower feeling like a well-loved woman. Noah had made very good use of all the architectural features of her shower. He'd caressed her and washed her and kissed her all over her body; he had made her feel bold and womanly in a way that no other man had done before. Not only had he pleased her completely, worshipping her with his hands and his fingers and his lips, but she had felt confident enough to return the favor. Honestly, she would never be able to see her shower bench in the same light again.

"Do you want a glass of wine?" she asked Noah, who was lingering in the hot shower.

"Sure."

Shayna walked into the bedroom, slipped into her robe and was about to head to the kitchen when she heard his phone ring.

"Answer it," he said when she said it was an overseas call.

So, she picked up the phone.

"Hello?"

"Put Major Brand on the phone."

"Major Brand?" she asked.

"That's right. Major Brand," the man on the other end of the line said tersely. "Is he there?"

Shayna covered the speaker on the cell phone and said in a harsh whisper, "Someone is asking for Major Brand?"

"Major?" Noah had shut off the water and was drying himself off with a towel.

She nodded and handed him the phone.

"Captain Brand speaking."

Shayna stood in the doorway of the bathroom and listened carefully, but she wasn't able to make out the words on the other end of the line.

"Yes, sir," Noah said. "Thank you, sir."

"What?" she asked anxiously after he hung up. "Who was that?"

Noah stared at his phone as if it held the answer to her questions. Then he looked up with a peculiar expression on his face. "That was Colonel Love."

Shayna raised her eyebrows in anticipation.

"You're not going to believe this, Shay. I can hardly believe it," Noah told her. "I've got new post orders."

Her entire body tensed as if to protect her from whatever he was about to say.

"I've been promoted to major."

"That's incredible, Noah." Her arms crossed. "I'm so happy for you."

"Be happy for *us*, Shay," he said. "I've got new orders. I'm going to be the commander in charge of recruiting in Bozeman."

Shayna's hands covered her mouth; her eyes widened. "Are you serious?"

"I'm coming home, my love." Noah reached for her and folded her securely into his arms. "I get to be with you, I get to be a father to Isabella and I still get to be a marine."

"Will you be home for Christmas, Noah?" Tears of happiness and relief spilled onto her cheeks and, for once, she didn't try to stop them.

"Yes, my love." He kissed her tears away. "I'll be home for Christmas."

Chapter Sixteen

Shayna was grateful that she had so much work to keep her busy. Noah returned to Japan to transition from his overseas post to his new job assignment in Bozeman and pack up his apartment. They video chatted every day, but it wasn't the same as having him with her; she could hear him—she could see him—but she couldn't touch him or breathe in the scent of his skin. So, she threw herself into decorating the house, installing the freshly painted princesses and planning to string the thousands of lights it would take to make the display come to life. She was also digging into research for her book, exercising with Blake and painting.

"Hi, Annika!" Shayna greeted Isabella's mother at the door.

"Hi, Shayna." Annika held out a bag of ornaments. "May wanted you to have these."

Shayna took the plastic bag, curious. She looked inside and found handmade ornaments that she had made for May's Christmas tree. Shayna touched each weathered and delicate ornament with reverence.

"I can't believe she kept these for all these years," Shayna finally said when she was able to speak.

"She keeps everything." Annika rolled her eyes. "I just hope Bella doesn't become a pack rat, too."

Every time Shayna saw Annika, she looked better— today she was wearing workout clothes, her hair was washed and pulled back into a neat ponytail, and her eyes were bright and clear.

"Do you want to come in?" she asked.

Annika hesitated and then said, "Maybe for a minute."

Once inside the house, her guest stopped to take in the decorations. "It's like stepping into a Christmas store."

"Thank you!" Shayna said with a broad smile. When she couldn't sleep for missing Noah, she worked on unpacking and putting up her decorations. The stockings were hung, the music boxes were lovingly placed on end tables and she had an enormous wreath above the fireplace that was covered in crystal Christmas trees and red velvet bows.

"Help me hang these?" she asked Annika.

"You don't have to," her guest said. "You could toss

them into the trash and May wouldn't know the difference."

"Are you kidding? I *want* to hang them."

Annika helped her hang her pine-cone ornaments by the faded and frayed green yarn that Shayna had attached so many decades ago. There was a pine-cone Santa, a pine-cone Frosty and a pine-cone Christmas tree.

"I'm so grateful to have them." Shayna admired the ornaments that they had hung on the tree by the front door. These silly little ornaments were more precious to her than the most expensive in her expansive collection. "It means a lot."

Annika had her hands in the pockets of her workout jacket. "You and Mom always had that in common."

"Do you want a cup of coffee?" Shayna asked.

"Okay."

Annika sat down at the kitchen island, and Shayna poured two cups of coffee.

"You know—" Shayna held the warm cup between her hands "—when we were kids, I was always so jealous of you."

"Me?" Annika seemed genuinely surprised.

Shayna took a sip of her coffee. "You always had a beautiful Christmas tree and so many presents. May always baked Christmas cookies, and you got to have a huge family Christmas meal."

Annika gave a little shrug of her shoulders. "I was jealous of you."

"Me?" Shayna said with the same genuine surprise.

"What in the world did I have that made you feel jealous?"

Annika had been popular and pretty and athletic. She had been the homecoming queen and a state champion to boot. And, most importantly, she'd had Noah.

Annika put her cup down; she was looking into the coffee when she said, "Mom was always saying, 'Why can't you be more like Shayna? She helps me in the kitchen, she helps me with the chores…'"

"Only because I didn't want to be at home alone," she interjected.

"Noah always talked about you." Annika frowned. "Shayna this and Shayna that. I honestly just got sick of hearing your name."

Shayna had to admit that it had never occurred to her, not even once, that Annika was jealous of her.

"Noah did the same thing to me," she told Annika.

Her guest nodded before she finished off her coffee. "I'd better be going. I'm going to be working out with Blake again."

Shayna took the empty cups and put them in the sink. "How's that going?"

At the door, Annika paused. "I'm glad you put me in contact with him. I haven't worked out in years, and it feels really good to be back in the gym."

"And how is everything else going?"

"You mean with my sobriety?"

Shayna nodded.

"It's a battle every day to stay clean," Annika admitted bluntly. "Sometimes it's every second of every day.

But I'm working the program—I'm attending meetings. I'm taking it one day at a time. I have Isabella."

"I believe in you, Annika," Shayna said. "You might not have been born here, but you're Montana tough now."

Annika gave her the briefest of smiles. "Thank you, Shayna. You've been really…kind to me. And you've been good to my daughter."

"Well, that's the easy part."

"For you, maybe," Annika countered as she walked through the open door. "But not for most people."

"Make sure you tell May thank you."

"I will." Annika paused at the end of the walkway. "She's back up on her feet and has one of those walkers to help her get around. Just as ornery as ever."

Shayna waved one last time before she shut the door. Right when she closed the door, her phone rang. She pulled it out of her back pocket to see who was calling. It was Noah!

"Hi!" Shayna answered the phone. She sat down on the nearby couch and curled her legs to the side.

"Hi, my love."

"It's so good to hear your voice."

"It's good to hear your voice," he said, but she detected something off in his tone.

"What's wrong?"

"I hate that I have to tell you this, but I'm not going to be home in time for the Marine Corps Ball."

Shayna's body froze at the news. "Oh."

Every year, the US Marine Corps celebrated its birth-day on November 10. Balls were held all over the coun-try, but getting a ticket to the Marine Corps Ball in Washington was like winning a golden ticket to Willy Wonka's chocolate factory—it was a big deal. And Col-onel Love, Noah's angel as far as she was concerned, had given him tickets to attend. With Lee's help, she had bought the most amazing gown, shoes and a spar-kly clutch that resembled a Fabergé egg.

"I'm sorry," Noah said. "I know how much you were looking forward to it."

Shayna swallowed hard a couple of times and cleared her throat to dislodge a hard question she needed to ask. "Does this mean that you won't be home for Christ-mas, Noah?"

"No," he reassured her, "I promise I'll be home for Christmas."

Yes, she wanted to go to the ball with Noah and dress up in her figure-flattering dress and stay in a fancy hotel in the nation's capital. She had longed to go to the prom with Noah; a ball in Washington seemed like an incredible upgrade. But the most important thing to her was that Noah was going to be home before Christmas.

"I have to go, sweetheart," he said. "I love you."

"I love you."

"Where are you going to hang these, Shayna?" Lee asked, holding sprigs of mistletoe in her hands.

Lee had come over to help her with the finishing

touches in the house—the first week of December would be the soft opening of her yard installation. The local newspaper and TV stations would be attending the soft opening, and she was now in a frantic rush to make everything as perfect as she could.

"Here, I'll take care of these if you'll watch the cookies."

This year, she was going to let people buy tickets to tour the house—the proceeds would go to a charity that helped homeless women with children find stable homes and employment. Shayna put the first sprig of mistletoe in the entryway to the formal living room and the second sprig in the doorway leading into her art studio. She was just climbing down from the step stool when the doorbell rang. Pilot, ever the faithful watchdog, lifted his head up from his downy pillow and let out three very distinctive woofs.

"That's probably Colt wondering if I'm ever coming home!" Lee said with a bright smile. "Junior's been giving us a real run for our money lately."

Shayna trotted over to the door, her ponytail swinging as she moved. She swung open the door.

"Hello, my love."

"Noah?" she exclaimed as she hurled herself into his arms. "What are you doing here? I wasn't expecting you so soon!"

Noah lifted her up in his arms so her feet were no longer touching the ground. "I'm surprising you."

Noah lowered her to the ground, took the mistletoe from her fingers, held it over their heads and kissed her with all the pent-up passion of a man who had been away from his woman for far too long.

"Are you surprised?" he asked, his eyes locked with hers.

"I'm floored," she said and kissed him again.

Arm in arm they walked together through the front door.

"Lee!" Shayna said. "Look who's here!"

"Hi, Noah."

"Hi, Lee." Noah kept his arm firmly around Shayna's waist. "Is everything ready?"

Shayna's eyes bounced from Noah to her friend and back to Noah. "Is *what* ready?"

Lee had a huge Cheshire-cat grin on her face.

"Wait a minute." Shayna pointed to Lee. "Why aren't you surprised that Noah's here?"

Instead of answering her, Lee disappeared down the hallway.

"What's going on?" Shayna asked Noah.

"You'll see."

Lee reappeared, rolling a suitcase behind her with a garment bag folded over her arm.

"Is that my suitcase?"

"I packed for you," Lee said.

Shayna looked up at Noah's face; he seemed very pleased with himself. "It looks like we're going to the Marine Corps Ball after all."

Shayna had never been *whisked away* on a surprise romantic getaway, but she was totally into it. Lee had already planned to watch Pilot, and the house and yard display were ahead of schedule, so she could afford to take some time for herself and Noah. It wasn't in her nature to be spontaneous, but being with Noah made her want to get out of her comfort zone.

Noah had hired a limousine to take them to the airport, where his sister-in-law's private family jet was awaiting their arrival. Once they landed, another limousine took them to the hotel, where Noah had booked a glorious suite for them. They made love late into the night before they ordered a late-night snack from room service and then fell asleep in each other's arms, satiated, full and exhausted. The next day, Noah had booked an appointment for her at the hotel spa—she got a facial, a massage and a mani-pedi. She returned to the room feeling pampered and ready for a nap. When she awakened, Noah had returned from his workout in the gym. They ordered room service, ate lunch in the room, and then it was time to get ready for the ball.

"One more surprise," Noah said when there was a knock on the door.

"No, Noah. You've already done too much."

Noah shook his head, "I could never do too much for you."

"Where should I set up?" A twenty something girl was at the door; she walked into the hotel room carrying two large, overstuffed bags on each shoulder.

"You hired a makeup artist for me?" Shayna asked.

Noah winked at her with a smile. All Shayna could

do was hug him; reality was more magical than any of her most elaborate dreams.

"Thank you." She punctuated her words with a kiss. "I don't remember ever feeling this happy."

"You deserve it," Noah said before he disappeared into the smaller bedroom to get himself ready for the ball.

Noah took one last look at himself in the mirror. He was wearing his dress blues for the first time as a major. He stuck his hand into his pants pocket, pulled out a small velvet box and opened it to check the contents inside. Tonight, he would officially ask Shayna to marry him—he wanted everything to be perfect for her. He wanted her to have the most memorable proposal; he wanted to give her a story that she would tell, over and over again, to their children and their grandchildren.

Noah went into the main living area of the suite and waited for his love to appear. He checked his phone several times—it seemed like time was ticking by at a snail's pace. He swayed back and forth, not feeling like sitting or surfing on his phone. He just wanted to see Shayna.

The door to the master bedroom opened, and there Shayna stood in an elegant forest green ball gown that was cinched at the waist and followed the curve of her hips before it flared out. One of her most beautiful assets, her full, natural breasts, were tastefully showcased with off-the-shoulder straps and a sweetheart neckline.

"My God, Dr. Wade." Everything but Shayna faded into the background for him. "You are stunning."

Shayna smiled so brightly at him; the makeup artist had used a light hand and her hair was swept up into a twist, leaving long tendrils framing her face.

"I feel like I've just had a very *Pretty Woman*, Julia Roberts montage moment in there." Shayna seemed to glide across the floor toward him. She stopped before him, her hand on her stomach and a self-effacing expression on her face. "I can't take a full breath with these Spanx. But is breathing really all that necessary?"

Noah escorted her through the hotel lobby; he noticed men and women admiring Shayna, and he felt like the luckiest man. She was beautiful, kind, incredibly sweet, so intelligent and loyal.

"Are you having a good time?" he asked her on the ride to the ball.

"Are you kidding me?" She laughed, her hand resting on his arm. "I keep waiting for this limo to turn into a pumpkin."

He reached for her hand, his thumb moving over the spot where his ring would soon sit. Because he had known Shayna for most of his life, he knew what she liked—he knew what would move her—and he was certain that he had found the perfect engagement ring for her.

At the ball, Noah swept her into his arms and was able to lead.

"Noah Brand!" Shayna's eyes widened. "When did you learn how to dance?"

"I've practiced a bit," he boasted but then immediately stepped on her foot. Instead of getting upset, Shayna laughed it off, and that made him laugh, too.

"I suppose I need a bit more practice," he said sheepishly.

"You're doing great." Shayna always wanted to bolster his confidence. "I'm having the time of my life."

When there was a pause in the music, and Shayna's eyes were shining with happiness and her face was a lovely shade of pink from the dancing, Noah took the ring box out of his pocket and got down on one knee.

When Shayna realized what was happening, her hand came up to cover her mouth. He heard the murmuring of the marines and their dates nearby, but he was entirely focused on Shayna.

"Dr. Shayna Wade," Noah asked, opening the box, "would you do me the great honor of being my wife?"

Shayna nodded her head yes, and the crowd around them erupted with cheers, whistles and the loud sound of clapping hands.

He stood up, took her hand and slipped the antique platinum ring onto her finger. The center stone was a two-carat emerald surrounded by brilliant high-quality diamonds. Shayna loved the Victorian era and had always wanted a colored gemstone, not a diamond, for the center stone of her engagement ring.

"Oh, Noah." Shayna had tears in her eyes. "Don't make me cry! I'll ruin my makeup."

Noah pulled a monogrammed handkerchief out of his pocket, but, at the same time, Shayna also pulled a handkerchief from the hidden pockets in the skirt of her gown. He remembered a time when he'd given Shayna a handkerchief. It was the day she'd dropped him off at the airport—it was the day when they shared, however brief, their first kiss.

"You've had that all of these years."

Shayna pressed the handkerchief into the corner of her eyes to stop the happy tears from forming. She tucked it back into her pocket. "Of course. You've always been my guy."

As the music began to play, Noah swept his fiancée into his arms and led her around, to the best of his limited ability, the dance floor. He even managed to execute a dip or two.

Midway through the night, they decided to leave the ball and go back to the hotel. Noah could sense that Shayna wanted to have him all to herself, and he felt exactly the same way about her. On the way back to their hotel, Shayna said, "This is the most beautiful ring I've ever seen, Noah. It's perfect for me."

Noah dipped his head toward her with a pleased smile. "Do you know what else is perfect for you?"

She shook her head, tilting her head slightly so he could easily kiss her lips.

"Me," he murmured and then kissed his fiancée for the very first time.

Back at the hotel, Noah helped Shayna out of her gown and took pleasure in unpinning her hair so it was loose and free. Shayna disappeared into the bathroom so she could wash the makeup off her face. Noah changed out of his uniform into pajama bottoms, forgoing the top of the pajamas because he knew how much Shayna liked to look at his chest and his abs. He popped the cork on a bottle of champagne that he had ordered for them and poured two glasses.

"You've thought of everything." Shayna emerged from the bathroom wearing one of the plush hotel bathrobes, her face freshly scrubbed.

He handed her a flute, they raised their glasses and he said, "To us."

"To us," Shayna echoed and then added, "May we always be as happy as we are tonight."

Noah took pleasure in stripping his fiancée out of her robe and caressing every inch of her sensual, curvaceous body. He had waited all night to see her like she was now, lying back on the crisp white sheets, looking delectable, wearing nothing but her emerald engagement ring. She reached out her arms for him. He covered her body with his, reveling in the fact that she was already so ready for him. He slid into her until they were joined completely, his sounds of ecstasy mingling with hers. He held her lovely face in his hands. "I'll love you forever, Shayna. For always."

She smiled so sweetly, her eyes drifting shut; he watched her, taking pleasure in the way she arched her neck and the little gasps she made when he was deep inside her. They rocked together, finding their rhythm, holding each other tightly, arms and legs intertwined, his lips kissing her neck, the mounds of her breasts and her lovely taut nipples until he felt her reach her peak. And then he let himself go so they could ride the crashing waves together as one bonded pair.

Noah lay next to his love; she was lounging back into a tall stack of pillows, her skin flushed and rosy from their lovemaking.

"Do you want to be a Christmas bride?" he asked her.

"Actually, I have always wanted to be a Christmas Eve bride."

"Why Christmas Eve?"

"The lights are beautiful at night, and the presents are still wrapped under the tree."

Noah placed his hand over her stomach, wondering what Shayna would look like if she were pregnant with his child.

"Big wedding? Small wedding?"

"Small. Intimate."

"This year?" He caught her eye. "Next year?"

"This year."

Noah threaded his fingers with hers. "I want to give you babies."

"I want your babies." There was no hesitation in her answer.

"When?" he asked.

Shayna curled her body toward him so she could look into his eyes and he could look into hers.

"Now," she said. "As soon as possible. I'm not getting any younger, and neither are my eggs."

Noah frowned. "I wish I had figured all of this out years ago. We've lost so much time."

Shayna put her hand lovingly on his face. "Let's not live in regret, Noah. We're here now. That's all that really matters."

"We could've had a family by now."

"But we wouldn't have Isabella. I wouldn't want to miss her for the world."

"Thank you. I wouldn't, either." Noah captured her hand and kissed it and then held it over his heart. "I love Isabella…"

"I know you do…"

"But maybe I wasn't supposed to be there when she was a baby," he said quietly, thoughtfully. "Maybe I was supposed to experience that with you."

Noah kissed Shayna, and even though they had just made love, his body wanted more. Shayna felt his growing desire for her, moved her head back so she could look into his face.

"Already, Major Brand?" she asked with a sweet laugh.

"Well, Dr. Wade," he said as he gently pressed her back into the thick mattress. "You did say that you wanted to get started *now*."

Epilogue

Shayna married Noah Brand on Christmas Eve. It was a small affair with close friends and family attending. The wedding was held at Shayna's house; it seemed the perfect setting for Christmas Eve nuptials. After the ceremony, the caterers set up tables in the main living room so the guests could dine surrounded by mistletoe, Christmas trees, lights, wreaths and giant Santa candles that smelled just like a candy cane.

After they cut the cake, the guests left and the caterers thankfully cleaned up, the three of them got ready for the final event of the night. Shayna had never had family traditions that she had carried from childhood into her adulthood, but to her mind, it was never too late to start.

"Are the matching pajamas *really* necessary?" Noah came out sporting red flannel Santa pajamas.

"Uh, *yeah*." She laughed, "They are totally necessary. And you look super handsome in those Santa jammies."

Isabella skipped into the room wearing a matching set of pajamas and then slid onto her knees in front of the Christmas tree. She pulled a green bow off one of the presents and put it on Pilot's head.

"That's better," Isabella said and hugged the Great Dane, who was tired from all the activity in the house.

"This is the beginning of our Christmas traditions," Shayna said. "On Christmas Eve, we will sing Christmas carols and drink hot cocoa with marshmallows, all while wearing matching Christmas pajamas…"

"And we get to open *one* gift!"

"That's right," Shayna confirmed. "One gift."

Noah brought a large box that had been hidden in a closet and set it down in front of Isabella. "I think you should get us started, Isabella."

Isabella bounced up with excitement and began to tear off the bows, ribbon and wrapping paper. She pulled open the top of the box and yelled, "It's a saddle! It's my very own saddle!"

"Oh, Noah, it's beautiful," Shayna said when he lifted it out of the box. "It's fit for a princess."

"You'd better check the box," Noah said to his daughter. "There might be something else in there."

Isabella folded her body in half and dived into the

tall box. She dug through the Styrofoam popcorn until she found an envelope.

"I think this might be violating the one-present rule." Shayna raised an eyebrow at him.

"One box, one present." He grinned at her.

Isabella opened the envelope and pulled out a picture. "It's a horse."

The young girl seemed understandably less excited about the picture. But Noah was quick to explain, "It's not just *any* horse. That's *your* horse."

Isabella's eyes widened, and her mouth dropped open. "It's *my* horse?"

"He's out at Sugar Creek, and he'll be there any time you want to see him."

Isabella flung herself into his arms, and Shayna was grateful that she was able to witness this incredibly special Christmas surprise with her husband and her daughter.

"Look, Shayna." Isabella ran over to her and showed her the picture. "This is *my* horse."

"He's a beauty," Shayna said and gave her a hug. "You're a lucky girl."

Noah moved some boxes around, and there, hidden beneath the other presents, was a small gift. He handed it to her.

"Merry Christmas Eve, wife."

Shayna opened the box and found earrings and a necklace that were a perfect match for her engagement ring. So grateful to be Noah's bride, Shayna had him help her put on the jewelry.

"They're lovely, Noah." She gave him a thank-you kiss. "Thank you."

"I'm glad you like them."

Shayna stood up. "Now it's your turn, Noah. I'll be right back."

She walked to her art studio and picked up a present in a thin, tall box. Returning, she set it down in front of her husband.

"What is this?" he asked, standing up so he could open the present.

"You'll have to open it to see."

Isabella joined them, curious to see what was beneath the wrapping paper.

Noah carefully slid a painting free from the box.

"Do you like it?" Shayna watched his face closely. It was a painting of Isabella in the backyard with Pilot. In the painting, Isabella was wearing the same outfit she had worn the day Noah met her.

"I don't know what to say, Shayna." Noah had tears in his eyes. "I love it."

"I helped!" Isabella bounced up and down excitedly.

"Yes, you did," Shayna said. "I couldn't have done it without you."

Noah put his arm around her shoulders and kissed her. "Thank you, Shayna."

"You're welcome." She smiled up at him. "But you'd better check that box before you start stuffing it full of wrapping paper. You're not the only person who can put two presents in one box."

Noah went back to the box and fished out an envelope. Shayna stood by, watching and waiting, doing her best to keep her secret for just a couple of seconds more.

Noah opened the envelope, pulled out a black-and-white photograph, and studied it. When he finally looked up at her, she couldn't hold it in any longer.

"You got your wish, Noah." She had her hands over her stomach. "We're pregnant."

Wordlessly, with tears of pure happiness and joy in his ocean-blue eyes, Noah pulled her into his embrace and whispered, "*You* are my Christmas wish, Mrs. Brand. Everything else is just a beautiful bonus."

* * * * *

Want more single parent romances? Try these other great books from Harlequin Special Edition:

The Spirit of Second Chances
By Synithia Williams

Forever, Plus One
By Wendy Warren

Lessons in Fatherhood
By Makenna Lee

Available now wherever Harlequin Special Edition books and ebooks are sold!

#2941 THE CHRISTMAS COTTAGE
Wild Rose Sisters • by Christine Rimmer

Alexandra Herrera has her whole life mapped out. But when her birth father leaves her an unexpected inheritance, she impulsively walks away from it all. And now that she's snowed in with West Wright, she learns that lightning really *can* strike twice. So much, in fact, that the sparks between them could melt any ice storm...if only they'd let them!

#2942 THANKFUL FOR THE MAVERICK
Montana Mavericks: Brothers & Broncos • by Rochelle Alers

As a rodeo champion, Brynn Hawkins is always on the road, but something about older, gruff-but-sexy rancher Garrett Abernathy makes her think about putting down roots. As Thanksgiving approaches, Brynn fears she's running out of time, but she's determined to find her way into this calloused cowboy's heart!

#2943 SANTA'S TWIN SURPRISE
Dawson Family Ranch • by Melissa Senate

Cowboy Asher Dawson and rookie cop Katie Crosby had the worst one-night stand ever. Now she's back in town with their two babies. He won't risk losing Katie again—even as he tries to deny their explosive chemistry. But his marriage of convenience isn't going as planned. Maybe it's time to see what happens when he moves his captivating soul mate beyond friendship...

#2944 COUNTDOWN TO CHRISTMAS
Match Made in Haven • by Brenda Harlen

Rancher Adam Morgan's hands are full caring for his ranch and three adorable sons. When his custody is challenged, remarriage becomes this divorced dad's best solution—and Olivia Gilmore doesn't mind a proposal from the man she's loved forever. But Adam is clear: this is a match made by convenience. But as jingle bells give way to wedding bells, will he trust in love again?

#2945 SECRET UNDER THE STARS
Lucky Stars • by Elizabeth Bevarly

When his only love, Marcy Hanlon, returns, Max Tavers believes his wish is coming true. But Marcy has different intentions—she secretly plans to expose Max as the cause of her wealthy family's downfall! She'll happily play along and return his affections. But if he's the reason her life went so wrong, why does being with him feel so right?

#2946 A SNOWBOUND CHRISTMAS COWBOY
Texas Cowboys & K-9s • by Sasha Summers

Rodeo star Sterling Ford broke Cassie Lafferty's heart when he chose a lifestyle of whiskey and women over her. Now the reformed party boy is back, determined to reconnect with the woman who got away. When he rescues Cassie and her dogs from a snowstorm, she learns she isn't immune to Sterling's smoldering presence. But it'll take a canine Christmas miracle to make their holiday romance permanent!

So that was an option, just to say that she needed her alone
time and West would intrude on that. Everyone would
understand. But then he would stay at the Heartwood Inn
and that really wasn't right...

And what about just telling everyone that it would be
awkward because she and West had shared a one-night
stand? There was nothing unacceptable about what she
and West had done. No one here would judge her. Alex
and West were both adults, both single. It was nobody's
business that they'd had sex on a cold winter night when
he'd needed a friend and she was the only one around
to hold out a hand. It was one of those things that just
happen sometimes.

It would be weird, though, to share that information
with the family. Weird and awkward. And Alex still
hoped she would never have to go there.

"Alex?" Weston spoke again, his voice so smooth and deep and way too sexy.

"Hmm?"

"You ever plan on answering my question?"

"Absolutely." It came out sounding aggressive, almost angry. She made herself speak more cordially. "Yes. Honestly. There's plenty of room here. You're staying in the cottage. It's settled."

"You're so bossy…" He said that kind of slowly— slowly and also naughtily—and she sincerely hoped her cheeks weren't cherry red.

"Weston." She said his name sternly as a rebuke.

"Alexandra," he mocked.

"That's a yes, right?" Now she made her voice pleasant, even a little too sweet. "You'll take the second bedroom."

"Yes, I will. And it's good to talk to you, Alex. At last." Did he really have to be so…ironic? It wasn't like she hadn't thought more than once of reaching out to him, checking in with him to see how he was holding up. But back in January, when they'd said goodbye, he'd seemed totally on board with cutting it clean. "Alex? You still there?"

"Uh, yes. Great."

"See you day after tomorrow. I'll be flying down with Easton."

"Perfect. See you then." She heard the click as he disconnected the call.

HARLEQUIN
PLUS

Announcing a **BRAND-NEW** multimedia subscription service for romance fans like you!

Read, Watch and Play.

Experience the easiest way to get the romance content you crave.

Start your **FREE 7 DAY TRIAL** at
<u>www.harlequinplus.com/freetrial</u>.